Locus Amoenus

LOCUS AMOENUS

V. N. ALEXANDER

Permanent Publishing

NY, NY

Library of Congress Cataloging-in-Publication Data

Alexander, V. N.

Locus Amoenus/Victoria N. Alexander

ISBN: 978-1-68994365-9 (softcover)
1. 9/11 novel   2. political satire
3. literary fiction   I. Title

for Lucian Rex

Preface

I have always felt that being involved in national politics is a great waste of time. The f that either red or blue can come up with about equal probability in most elections leads me to suspect that the decision is really a thoughtless coin toss, a mere muscular reaction, a twitch. When I had a free moment, I promised myself, I'd get involved locally, at the radical root of democracy, where I might be able to do something. A few years ago, I made an effort in the rural New York hamlet where my family owns a farm. And now I know that corruption and conspiracy are not to blame so much as the meaner diseases of complacency and conformity. I groan at the prospect of taking on this subject, with which I would much rather have nothing to do.

-V.N.A.

Prologue

Chapter One
Et in Amenia

As you drive northeast through Dutchess County in upstate New York, farm scenes strike calendar poses: leaning barns, well-tended white Victorians, winding roads tunneling through overhanging maples. Then, round a bend, a vista breaks open upon hilly patchwork fields and cow-dotted pastures, with many layered hills growing progressively mistier in the farther distance. This stretch of the Harlem Valley is none other than the very *locus amœnus* of pastoral paradise, where nothing bad can ever happen.

My mother and I moved here from Brooklyn at the end of 2002. We didn't feel safe in the city anymore, and we could no longer bear the fact that every time we heard an uneven tread in the stairway, we thought it might be Dad finally coming in the door. We supposed removing ourselves from the familiar physical triggers would help extinguish that cruel hope reflex.

This morning, instead of taking the bike path past the train station, I decided to run up DeLaVergne Hill to look down upon the hamlet Amenia, whose name means "pleasing to the eye." From up here I can soliloquize to the greatest advantage about the larger perspectives necessary to frame my story. We may take Amenia for what it is: a miniature in enamel, hung from a gold chain around a virgin's neck, an abstract of the times.

The last stop on the train from the city, it lies as far as one might retreat into rural country without losing that connection to urbanity. In this valley an abandoned length of rail bed, which used to route the train on up into Massachusetts, is now a bike path. It cuts through shale cliffs —hung over with fern and dripping moss—and then snakes languidly through swamps, woods, and sheep pasture. Sometimes opening wide and scenic, sometimes growing close and shady, the "rail trail" is nevertheless boycotted by the locals, who, years before, fought bitterly against the intrusive charity that would convert and maintain it. They feared youth would be drawn to the asphalt surface late at night for Colt 45 drinking parties. But they have been proven wrong, and the rail trail is used mostly by the bottled-water crowd, human-billboard cyclists and new moms chasing three-wheeled strollers who come up from the city to their weekend homes. The locals despise these people whom they call "citiots," exhibiting an otherwise unprecedented stroke of cleverness.

A sign at the entrance to the rail trail promises that "no motorized vehicles" are allowed, but local forces lobbied and affixed a second sign further announcing that the trail is "patrolled by sheriffs on ATV's" [sic]. We can say that the signs agree to disagree for now. One idea of respect is to avoid making a choice. The smaller guy is moved by tolerance, the other by pride.

Here it comes now—following its own deep, pulsating sonic wave—a pimped-out, camo-painted, all-terrain vehicle, complete with a custom stereo system louder than the engine. The funds for its requisition, I hear, came from some unusual interpretation of a line in the sheriff department's Homeland Security budget. Atop this fantastic vehicle, a large-faced deputy reigns, swooshing past startled cyclists and waking babies with his thunder. He heads down the rail trail toward a parking area where four men stand talking around the bed of a pickup, the redneck conference table. The deputy pulls up and dismounts speaking to the men. Simultaneously, all heads turn to look up the hill to where I stand looking down at them.

I start back toward our farm, where my mom and I have lived happily enough for almost seven years, sporadically, between trips abroad and cross-country. With the insurance settlement, we bought our farm from a vegan woman whose unrealistic wool business had failed. We are among numerous other well-heeled former urbanites, "living off the land" within convenient reach of the train to New York City and equidistant from five tolerably decent airports.

But things are not quite as peaceful at home as they could be. Of late, sorry to say, an "uncle Claudius" has interloped, got in between my fortune and me. He executed the move just last month when I was away at school. Not really an uncle, but "stepdad" won't do. Today is the wedding. Our lawn is crawling with caterers, and the musicians are setting up even now. Will I still sit at the head of the table tomorrow? He has been eyeing my seat these last couple of days since I have been home, but I make a point to get to the table early to claim it. I think he even may

3

have occupied it while I was gone. I found my seat unpleasantly warm. But my name, alongside my mother's, was still on the parcel map last time I looked, and I mean to keep it that way. Our home was dearly bought.

Our cottage is very old, circa 1750. It first appears in the records in 1763 when it acquired a new porch. How long it had stood porchless we can only guess a decade or two. It has been added to and upon in every direction over the years and currently has the structure of a human hive of some sort, mostly done up in Quaker-gone-Tudorish, crumbling here and there, sagging a little now and again. But it's lovely and storybook; a stranger can get lost in passageways and cupboards. In our old house, we know none of the mean evenness of imported fruits and machine weather. We eat in season and hang the laundry. All these years we have followed Voltaire's advice, my mother and I. We have twenty-two horned, long-haired wild-looking sheep of small size— in various colors from dirty white, to chestnut, to shoe black —the ewes about that of a big retriever and the rams and wethers not much larger. With slender legs and two-pronged toes, they step lightly over the rock outcroppings in our hilly pasture. In the spring before shearing season, the ewes' overgrown coats make them look like tiny Jewish grandmothers who got their furs four sizes too big at a thrift shop. They roam around the cottage lawn and occasionally, if the door has been left open, step inside, clattering over the floorboards, sounding as if a crowd of high-heeled ladies has just arrived.

On a quiet morning when sheep shake off the frosty dew, the wool rumbles like distant thunder. I can distinguish the tenor of their bleats. Some ewes are plaintive or begging, some are rude and angry. Pluto, the lead ram, a sturdy black animal, is mostly silent, but when he does speak, it is like a kitten mewing. There is a worn and polished fence post he scratches his woolly face against for hours, and when I come to the barn in the morning with my shovel, he greets me, putting his head down so that I can get that spot behind his horns. He was good enough to give old Claudius a swift butt once, sending him face forward into a manure pile. Good Pluto.

At the age of twelve I became a full-time shepherd—who, true, has read more than roamed. I am an experiment. Some may claim "gone awry." My mother, after trying hard to do otherwise, educated me at home, where I read and read and read. Too many books and not enough interaction, says Claudius. My life has become one long self-conscious narration. My hours and days are pages turning, and I cannot wait to get to the end.

For the greater part of seven years, we have been more or less holed up from the thumb-communicating world. There are no malls in Amenia. One buys one's clothes at Tractor Supply, or else at the drug store. There are no billboards, and if one does not have cable TV, an aptly named Yahoo account, or newspaper subscriptions—and we do not—a lot of celebrity news can go on without one ever knowing about it. Sure, things come up in conversation, and, as we go through the grocery line we receive our inoculating dose of tabloid, but that is the extent of our exposure to the flotsam and jetsam that people take for information. As a child, I read the classics and liked math and science. I got very good at finding geeky things online and somehow missed everything else. You really can tunnel your way through the Internet using Scholar Google. Besides my flock, I had plenty of playmates, young and old, all over the world, but I completely slept through American popular culture, knowledge of which, it appears to me, could be as important as knowing last year's weather predictions.

Our house is one of several very old homes in the area, but most in town are much younger Victorians or prewar farmhouses that rose up in the boom of the Jewish resort beside the lost Amenia lake, whose dam broke and flooded the poor goys in Wassaic below. A hundred years of no development ensued, and then, slowly, a grave state psychiatric prison hospital was erected on the hill, calling forth thousands of low-paid workers from the north and spawning trailer parks and split-ranch tragedies, spreading sprawl even here, where Lewis Mumford lived, where for the longest time, town and farm refused to produce the monstrous progeny suburb. Now every Sunday the automaton locals, on stinky noisy mowers, go meticulously back and forth across their great tartan plains.

Happily, suburban expansion was limited. The state facility closed after sixty or so years of operation; atrophy replaced growth; the grand old hotel and other treasures were burned to the ground by a few local delinquents. Then, post 9/11, as small dairy farmers' suicides were being subsidized by various federal farm bills, citiot migration really began in earnest. The former pederast house was converted into eco-condominiums with equestrian amenities. Failed farms were bought up by the uber wealthy who built stately manors, installed waterfalls, and imported gazelles and camels for their lawns.

In the meantime, however, the wave of workers from the north grew to far outnumber the settled farmers. These later folks became "the locals" but are themselves Adirondackian diaspora, whose weekend hunting plots, for reasons hidden to me, are *there* not here. Now that the state facility has closed down, released its residents into the population, the locals work hard at two, and sometimes three, part-time service jobs so that they can drive an hour to a Walmart to buy lots of plastic crap they don't need, get themselves deeper into debt, and pay their taxes—often with high interest credit cards—to support undeclared wars and to bail out banksters. They actually vote, right and left, to remain enslaved, instead of throwing off their partisan shackles, waving crowbars with half-articulate shouts of fury. When these NeoUncleToms die, I expect they will go straight to Terrordise, a celestial gated community where cavity searches are the routine safety procedure for all ages, all foodstuffs are engineered and radiated, and all information carefully filtered of meaningful content.

The locals don't hike the gorgeous hills that surround the valley; and they fought my mother to keep the trucked-in junk food for the school cafeteria instead of switching to locally grown vegetables. They actually encourage their girls to watch banal Disney romances, in which everyone seems to scream at each other at first and then marry at the end. They train their boys with video games to see slaughter as a form of entertainment.

Second- and third-homeowners now employ a good percentage of the locals—landscapers, carpenters, lawn mowers, snow plowers, pool cleaners, pest controllers, window washers, housekeepers, horse trainers, septic tank drainers, caterers, and tutors—whose own homes and families are left unattended. The grand estates wait in pristine readiness for their owners to visit while the landscaper's own vegetable garden is choked by weeds. There isn't a local in town who can afford to hire himself. The carpenter's own doors are sagging; the housekeeper's windows are opaque with dirt.

Polonius, my mother's friend, a short former military man with a large fortune and florid signature unfurling a full four inches, goes on about how the locals hate weekenders like himself: "If it weren't for us, whose homes would they take care of?"

Their own? Each other's? Maybe they would grow chard and raise chickens; maybe they would run little repair shops or make things to sell to one another; maybe they would not watch so many TV reality shows about grand estates whose lawns are mown by people like them.

Something is rotten in the United States of America.

Act I

9

Chapter Two
No More Marriages

All the wedding guests are dressed in virginal white, as are the musicians and the bridal party. The flowers, four-tiered cake, crisp table linens, billowing tent and pyramid of wrapped gifts are likewise white. Only a Hollywood director or my mother would or could enforce such aesthetic tyranny, painting this party scene on our cottage lawn. Everyone appears as dead-and-gone-to-heaven people do in movies and in dreams. A few uncooperative cousins arrived last night in beige, and Gertrude actually bleached clothes by moonlight. The sheep were segregated (Pluto and other darkies locked in the barn), and those that were sinfully grey were washed white as snow and set to grazing on the periphery, softly bah-ah-ing the sound of innocence as the forty-seven-year-old widow-virgin—Danish blonde hair mum on her true years, ivory skin scrubbed to poreless sheen —said she does to her junior by five years. He, also colorless, as well as humorless, said he does, and now we all seated are at long narrow tables arranged in a U, attacking cod and cauliflower.

Hamlet [dressed in black] sits with others at the head table.

Names have been changed to implicate the guilty.

"A toast," bellows Claudius, thrusting out his beer glass, "to my bride." Clink, clink, clink. Gertrude stupidly beams. It is one of those complex September late afternoons with a low, clear and bright sun stabbing through dark slate blue clouds at regular intervals, punching up primary color intensity of the green grass, red barn, and yellow wildflowers. Rain had threatened with increasing melodrama, but no one took it seriously. Finally, the great grey-bottomed ships weighed anchor and left a dazzling clear blue sky in their wake, and it started to grow hot.

Claudius, sweating exactly as much as his beer glass, stands at his place, with Gertrude looking up at him as she sits by his side. Like Gertrude, we may admire this man for his many negative qualities: he is not ambitious, he doesn't have a lot of money, he isn't any good at rhetoric. Although he has a PhD in engineering, he has a negative degree of knowledge about humanity. He can't quote even a doggerel verse to impress an audience, much less invent a good one to fit an occasion. Bad guys are usually good at poetry, in my experience, which makes them even more evil. Take Richard, for example. Not so with our Claudius. He lacks that extraordinary measure that evil men so often possess, and he, I am reluctant to admit, is probably neither wicked nor even corrupt, but just a common fool and knave. More positively one could say he is modest, a man of duty who won't complicate things for Gertrude.

"And to my son," mineuncle continues in his coarse way. Some embarrassed friend in the crowd coughs, and this time there are not nearly so many hearty clinks.

Hamlet the hero-fool—who shall be played by me—stone-faced with darting eyes, does not taste his white wine. I am not in a party mood. Ever since I returned from school, my clear-as-glass pool has been dredged up muddy, and all manner of unwanted memories like undecayed bodies from the cold preserving depths of denial have risen to the surface. With morbid fascination now I fish out the past, sometimes with cool dispassion and sometimes with warm briney waves of sorrow. Gauging the depth of the pain I feel now, clearly I hardly mourned before. It must have been merely a mourning exercise that my relatives and friends put me through—an inoculation against sorrow that didn't take, and now I am infected dangerously late in the day.

"Kind kismet turns our grief to gladness, pale fear to patriotic fury, confusion to confidence," Claudius prates on. "Were it not for the death of Hamlet *Senior*—in whose good character I believe and can only imitate to the best of my abilities—I would have never met my love," gulping. "The hand of fate looked upon a simple engineer, granting him the (probably undeserved) opportunity to serve his country in ways he never imagined." Here Gertrude fawns.

Could she really be proud of him, with the minor role he played in this universal drama that shook the foundations of soulless America?

" . . . to have been instrumental in answering the question of the horrible 'how,' incidentally for a whole nation and particularly for my new wife. We can now see clearly the path before us."

It had fallen to Claudius to apply his special knowledge of heat and stress in the investigation of the physical destruction of the twin towers. He was assigned to a particular type of bolt and spent many experimental hours with it. He, along with a compartmentalized team of government engineers, generated a hefty tome that concluded: fire is hot; steel weakens under stress and heat. Not exactly Nobel-Prize-winning science, but they meant merely to confirm what was so obviously true. The plane-damaged buildings caught fire and fell. Like all good bureaucrats, he generated a lot of paper, writ all over with measurements. What was measured mattered less than that there were many measurements taken. A set of data stood at the end, projecting an objectivity that no one, who was still awake, would question. Nevertheless, to Gertrude it seemed Claudius basked in the glow of one who had done real service for his country, as if he were one of those first responders who had tirelessly dug through rubble, working up lung disease, longing to find one body to bury.

September 11th changed the paths of many lives, and people who otherwise never would have met, and certainly never would have married, were thrown on a collision course, fated to initiate what Aristotle would approve of as a proper beginning, with causal chains thenceforth rattled and knotted in unexpected ways.

While Claudius helped mop up after the terror—in his own small way—my mother and I were victims of it, and it brought us all together. Terror started the wars and the Patriotism, capital P, the gathering behind the silly president, and made all criticism of government, even that one, mean and cheap.

It was a lot to be victims of all that. We carried upon us the blood and the burden of all that despair and desire for revenge. I am he for whom Afghani and Iraqi kids are losing their dads. For our sakes, armies launched.

How should the ordinary citizen interact with a symbol such as me, son of a murdered father? In elementary school, I was treated like the sacred cow. The other kids were reverent in my presence. That must have been troubling for them because they didn't care for me personally, meanwhile they had dads and uncles who were over there, fighting for me, some upstart come to live in their poor rural company with the insurance money. No, actually they probably never got that far in their analyses. They probably just felt uncomfortable with themselves and pitied and hated me for reasons they never examined.

All over the country, my mother and I were trotted out at many parties, fund-raising events mostly, where we were honored by a moment of silence, during which I too often inconveniently discovered I needed to cough. Sadly, after the special speech they didn't know what to do with us. When it came time to mingle, an empty space would form around us like a force field. Gertrude would whisper to me, *Here it comes.* The nearest person to us had just given us a pitying smile, and then, nodding her head at her empty glass, crept off toward the bar. The space she left behind her was not filled. A few people now looked across the growing bubble of empty floor, again with the pitying smiles. But who could blame them? We did not, for if they did cross that expanse, after they uttered their condolences and paid their respects, they would be stuck there with us, having nothing left to say, nothing appropriate or expressive of their sincerity (in which we never doubted), since our situation was beyond the imaginable. They felt like imposters in grief in our presence, for we were the real deal. We felt awkward and unwanted, like the ghosts of beloved relatives whose visits only spoil a good night's sleep.

It was at one of these functions that Claudius met Gertrude. Once again we were asked to stand for a moment of silence. This time the event centered on the congressional approval of funds to investigate the buildings' collapses. Once again, we stood alone and apart.

Claudius was there in official capacity, recently snatched out of the depths of academic obscurity to work on the report. He had all the advantages of our awkward circumstance. We were in our expanding bubble talking about nothing with each other. Claudius saw his moment. The rest shall be tedious history.

Flourish. We are still at the wedding.

"But to the future, we look now. Out of death comes new hope. We throw off our mourning and celebrate a new beginning, and to my new friends. And my son, who is not alone in paying duties to his father."

"Habit, sir," is my terse reply, a touch of correctness, an almost imperceptible twitch of the right brow.

"If it's a habit then that can be changed, like you can change your clothes. It's called 'moving on,' Dear," remarks Gertrude, not angrily.

"I am my habits. I could no more change them than I could stop being Hamlet."

"Your wearing black is a comment on my marriage," Gertrude whispers, leaning toward me, instructing by example.

I loud-whisper back, "A comment, good mother? No woman, it is a suggestion."

"She waited seven years and one year after that, per custom," adds Claudius, bowing to Gertrude.

"Very punctual," I say, blinking rapidly one, two, three times. It is a personal tic that incenses Gertrude. Auspiciously the band starts up with a strum, and the wedding party leaves the table for the dance floor.

Exeunt all but Hamlet.

"Eight years to the day, my mother remarries," I reflect aloud. "They couldn't pick a different number? A nice two? The twenty-seventh? That's a Sunday. *I* remember the eleventh. I remember. He wants to remake the day and she obeys, and I will be as black as I please. Today could have been the funeral we never had.

"Death in absentia? Not a splinter of bone nor a glob of flesh to bury or to burn. I would be off to the garbage dump today with wilting flowers, if I knew for certain he was scattered there. The Freshkills scavenger seagulls, hungry for more death and decay, flying overhead, vultures in different dress wailing like spoiled children.

"The honeymoon on the eleventh, with a fat engineer, a bureaucrat, a mercenary with a comb-over, muzzling her while she girlishly implores, 'Shh, we'll wake Hamlet.' And he, growling 'So what?' and banging his meaty palm on the headboard. Ah, but perfectly correct. All the forms observed."

Looking out beyond the tent, I see her sheep grazing scatteredly over the pasture. Even they are more independent than she. I can imagine how his dialog went: *We ought to do it this way. It's for the best. Put the past behind us. Look forward, not back.*

I remember the eleventh, the day he didn't come home.

I was at the foot of the Brooklyn Bridge. I saw a thundercloud billowing with black inside, pouring into all the empty spaces, curling around the buildings, enveloping the stranded cars and panicked ladies running in their high heels. There were fighter jets in the sky and the sun went dead, and I thought the enemy was above and war had begun.

I had been taking a field trip with my school, when our minibus got stuck in traffic downtown. My cousin

Bryant and I got out with the rest of the kids to look at the smoke rising out of the towers. When the cloud came, we didn't know what it was. We scattered. Dusty faceless strangers that seemed to only have eyes and mouths grabbed me and pushed me into a doorway. A fat lady and I cried together and hugged each other. Then people streamed by us across the bridge.

The papers would say the dust was like a dirty snowfall. It was like moondust. It was like nothing I had ever seen. There was an inch and a half of dust piled on a railing that I was standing near. I scooped some up with my hand. I pondered it for a long time, and after a while I realized my friend was gone, the fat lady with pillow bosom who had put her body between me and the cloud and said, "Sh, it's going to be okay. I'm here. I'm here."

She was an angel, probably, the way she came at the right moment and disappeared once I was safe. There probably are very fat angels. We don't realize it. Later, when I went watery-eyed some nights, I would imagine laying my head against her soft breasts while her mellow, low voice, said, "I'm here."

My science teacher, Mr. Horatio, found me, sitting on a rail, staring at the dust in my cupped hands, and he got my cousin and me home. That evening my mother and I listened to the news, wondering when my father would ring. We had no reason to think he had been at the World Trade Center. He was uptown at work. But most of the cell phones were down. We knew the trains weren't running, so when he didn't come home in the evening, we assumed he stayed with a friend. September 11th was the day I didn't know my father died. Didn't know for certain for several days, or rather we never knew for certain. He was one of the thousands of people who disappeared that day. Logic says he died there.

Maybe he had been on a train that had been blocked. Maybe he got out, and maybe he went into the building to help. We make up a story; it doesn't really have any details. He didn't die there and then, for me, he died when he didn't come home the second night. My experience as a victim was less real, a rumor, a fear, from the beginning. We didn't believe it, had no reason to, and we only just managed to convince ourselves later, my mother and I.

We are still at the wedding.

Enter Rosencrantz and Guildenstern in full-length white aprons quarreling. They begin to pick up the dishes as I pace the lawn beside the tent, with hands behind my back, bent like a monstrous crow. Coming up behind them, "Gentlemen," I startle them. I cannot keep from making mischief among the locals in Amenia.

"Hey Hamlet. Long Time," says Guildenstern.

Rosencrantz says nothing. His silences have a way of implying that he is resisting the temptation to dish out some especially nasty insult.

Nodding, "Rosencrantz. Guildenstern. Very long. Catering now is it?"

"Money's good."

"I bought a new truck."

"Lawn service done for the season then? We have the sheep do the mowing; the wind does the raking." I am not sure, as I speak, who is who, for men in Amenia may all like sports, but they never play them, and over the years, adding flesh, they grow more and more alike. Both are tall and overweight; their chests cage straining young hearts. They cannot live long.

Compared to them I have a rather feminine build, compared to them, that's key, about five foot ten, light on my feet. My black hair is long and lank and gets in my eyes.

Both G & R have fresh haircuts, as I remember they did always when they were boys, with clean-shaven necks, sideburns artfully shaped and pointing at their noses. They drove to Poughkeepsie for those haircuts once a fortnight. Their teeth are in shambles, and they talk like ventriloquists to hide them.

"You don't get that finished look," replies Guildenstern, or was it Rosencrantz, hardly moving his lips.

"The mower trails are missing, yes. That's Grandmother's Limoges. Break a piece and I shall have to take your truck."

Rosencrantz drops a bowl at my feet.

"Touché."

Guildenstern, unable to squash a grin, reveals evidence of the terrible mother who had suckled him on Coke and chocolate milk.

"Who's the old guy?" asks Rosencrantz of Polonius, who is dancing without partner, performing flourishes with grand waves of his arms and expressive wrist work.

"Friend of Mum's. Harmless, obviously."

We stand watching him. "He claims he was a colleague of Dad's. He showed up at the memorial and blew his nose louder than anyone else and insisted that he owed it to Dad to help us out. He's been something of a high-maintenance house pet since. But he does have a daughter."

"A daughter?"

"Yes, a daughter, at boarding school now. It was he who found our farm for us. He's got his own place in Millbrook. Horses. Ophelia likes to ride. She started early and is good at it. I haven't seen her yet, since I've been back, from school."

"College?" asks R.

"Of course, college. What, do you think he's going to trade school?" asks G.

"A trade is a good thing to have if you want to eat. But no I have no trade," I reply.

"When d'you get back?"

"Night before last, I arrived late by taxi with my dirty laundry."

The door was locked, and the house was dark, but there was a glow coming from the side. When I walked around, I saw it was coming from my window. There was Claudius through the glass, with paint roller attached to a long pole, glasses flecked with white paint, rolling over and over the ceiling to cover up the painted night sky and last trace of what was young Hamlet's room.

"I found him painting my old bedroom. He had moved out my stuff, and he was in, with his metal file cabinets, his black Formica desk and matching chair from the Staples catalog. His *red* ink pens, his organizers, his three-ring binders, his Wite-Out, his hefty desktop tape dispenser. God how can she stand it?"

"I suppose he has money."

"Suppose no such thing. She's a sucker. She's only doing it to be nice." I hissed the last word. "She can't say no to tragedy.

"But I cannot be mad at her for long. I went in, slept in the attic guest room with my exiled things. I got through the breakfast. But by noon, I was out. Moved to me old tree house out yonder," I say, pointing over my shoulder to an octagonal tower shot through with massive cottonwood limbs.

"The tree house," explodes Guildenstern with remembered excitement. "We slept there a few times."

"You would be right. With our sleeping bags and flashlights." A moment passes between G & R and me, as they stare at their feet and I bite my lip thinking, feeling my eyes fall into faraway focus. "And there am I happy. The roof is still tight, the urinal convenient in the middle of the night (open the window screen), and I can see him when he drives out the gate. So I can go in for breakfast and a shower," I add cheerfully.

"Hey, how long are you home for? We could go out get a few beers."

"Not quite like old times. I tell you what, gentlemen. Meet me in the tree house later, when the party begins to thin out. We'll try to stay up until midnight like before."

"We were what, twelve?"

"I think so. About that."

"Then your mom decided you were too good for school."

"That's what everyone says."

"That so? And do people care as well? Can't imagine that they would be interested in what Hamlet does."

"Well, your mom she's—"

An awkward silence follows that I prolong with a look of surprise. It is bad form on Rosencrantz's part. Not even rural hicks say things about one's mother. "At a loss for words?" I say smiling. "You know this whole town is something of a . . . Well, it doesn't matter."

Chapter Three
Queen, King

We sought refuge here knowing that even in arcadia there is tragedy, death, tooth decay, bad manners, and dollar stores, but sometimes one wants to trade in his given hardship for a fresh one. A hardship of one's own choosing is just the sort of thing to distract. The first several months in Amenia, Gertrude and I were insensitive to the fact we did not fit in, would never fit in, and would never want to anyhow, not once we found out what it was we were in. Unknown to us yet, some fatal faux pas had already fixed the outcome. Was it our foreign car? Or the way Gertrude answered, "I'm well," to the question, "How're you?" Was it that we used the rail trail? Or rode our bikes to the grocery store? Like Virgil's urbane poet, we had been keen to get on with the folk. We were so condescending our backs hurt, but they were not fooled.

Poor Gertrude. She meant well. She always means well. Tall, thin, nervous, awkward in affection, old fashioned in manners, she is very well meaning. In our former life in Brooklyn, she had had more than enough friends and donated at every empty coffee cup, every spread crushed-velvet cloth. Face firm, serious, thoughtful, Gertrude was perennially heading up this committee; volunteering at that charity; finding a new approach, a better theory. Very opinionated on virtually every subject, she also has a great tolerance for others. Consequently, she has several times been on the receiving end of the "one phone call" from down-going new acquaintances. She is drawn to broken people and dysfunctional community boards like a lawyer to an ambulance, a logician to a riddle. Give her something impossible to fix and her eyes drop to her lap, and she goes all quiet at dinner, and for days has something on her mind. Then finally, in the middle of the night, she is heard making a pot of coffee, tapping away at her computer, writing up a Letter to the Editor.

She has always clung tenaciously to the belief that understanding, communication, education can solve every social problem. As her son, I can say that she doesn't often stop to consider an emotion except when it's symptomatic of a lack of understanding on some point. When I was sad or angry about something, she set me next to her on the sofa and would explain, in a smooth cool voice, the whole concept underlying the issue, identify the problem and offer a practical solution. She bestowed her affection in her own way by giving me attention, and if I understood not a word of what she said, I was still calmed by the sound of her voice and her presence.

As a child I was comforted listening to her work compulsively through the night. I might wake from a nightmare craving her cool hand and soothing voice, but if she did not come, just hearing the tap, tap, tap on the keyboard or the pacing was comfort enough for me to fall back to sleep. She might forget to cook a meal or two for me. More than once I was handed a bowl of chickpeas out of a can, but while I ate, she would also tell me *all about* her project, make sure I understood the importance of the smallest detail, and sometimes even get me involved in some way. I might be called upon to secretly videotape a meeting with an unscrupulous CEO by pretending to play a cell phone game. Often I could sit on her lap as she read or talked on the phone or scribbled out notes. Always she took me to the meetings. Equipped with novels, a sketchpad, pencils, water and healthy snacks, I would get installed in reception areas (once at the governor's mansion) or at the far end of the conference table. Never did she ask permission or apologize for bringing me along. She acted as if it was her right, as a single mom, to parent at all times, everywhere.

She had breastfed me until I was three—restaurants, stores, parks, trains, strolling the streets—and the only reason she quit when she did is because her plane got rerouted on what was supposed to be an overnight trip. She spent three nights in a Chicago hotel while her breast pump gear had gone on ahead to New York. Her milk dried up. I believe I remember when she returned, all tears, huddling me to her robed breast. But I was fine. I was satisfied with fruits and vegetables.

No processed foods for me. Not a Cheerio, ever. She thwarted every potential health assault, carcinogens, poor aesthetics, television in general.

Naturally, Gertrude initiated the healing process immediately after my father died, mostly by keeping us busy. But it is an unpleasant thing to get over a death.

Her parenting eclipsed my father's. His memory barely peeks out around the edges of her moon. He was gone from early in the morning and came home just in time to put me to bed. I told him stories. At the age of three or four I started making up stories, a new one every night. I figure I made up about 2,737 original tales in all. They were short and turned on a clever pun or ironic reversal of fortune. How different things might be, how much more I would remember about him, if he had been the one to do the storytelling.

And here I am still, telling the story.

What do I recall of my father, sitting at the far end of my bed one leg folded on his knee? The smell of soap, an attentive smile. He was not a tall or in any way a physically impressive man. I remember big sad blue eyes and thick black hair—that's where I get my hair and eyes. He had a hawklike nose and his mother's weak chin. He was always very clean, like a doctor. He wore a tie that was loose by the time I saw him in it, but I imagine that it was tight and correct at dawn when he set out. He carried his suit coat but seldom wore it, even when it was chilly. The sole of his left shoe was a full inch and a half thicker than the sole of his right. He had his soft brown leather shoes custom-made at an Italian shop on a side street, and I went with him once to pick up a new pair.

I can still recall the Rockwellian scene, Dad sitting on the cobbler's stool, wriggling freed toes first before inserting them smoothly into the new pair. The proud artisan stood by, arms akimbo, beaming. My heart aches now to think he would have been called names in school and that somehow he had endured it. Maybe he wisely guessed the older he grew the less it would bother him. That day, with Tiny Tim happiness, he had so forgotten his misfortune that he was genuinely excited about the beauty of his fine new handicap shoes.

On the weekends, we would all get into the car and drive to some historical site. In the first ten years of my life, I visited every robber baron mansion, local museum, old mill, battlefield and historical marker in a three-hundred-mile radius around New York. In my memories of him, he is always consulting a map, guidebook, placard, directions to a site. There was usually some object of contemplation between us. We talked about Washington's crossing the Delaware, or we looked at the Huguenot houses in New Paltz, or wondered how the colonists had used some beautiful tool. I didn't talk much to my father about his boyhood in Missouri, or about his work. He was in industrial advertising and managed public relations for companies that manufactured mining equipment or sold explosives. I remember once I visited him at his office where he took time out in the midst of what seemed to be a crisis of some sort: people handing him papers, someone yelling into a phone. He grabbed his coat, which he didn't put on, and went out with Gertrude and me across the street to get an ice cream. While we slowly licked our cones, he forgot about the office and told us about the trip to the Allentown coal mine he had planned for later that week.

Bits and pieces of his boyhood came out occasionally in "when I was your age" mentions. He walked two miles to school, in knee-deep snow. His chores included making beer and cleaning the pigeon coop. His widowed mother and he ate squab. He earned a scholarship to Purdue, and his mother died while he was in his first year. He hitchhiked home in his funeral suit with a wooden suitcase (which I now have).

On one of our aimless trips across country in the summer months of 2002, Gertrude and I were passing through Joplin, and we stopped by the house where he grew up, a tiny blue 1920s bungalow situated on a tightly packed street. We got out of the car and approached a cheerful, enormous black woman who was mowing the lawn. We talked for a few moments and she said there were remnants of some kind of coop in the backyard. She led us through the gate to have a look, and there sunk in the lawn was the evidence of a concrete pier. We three stood hands clasped in front, heads down, a spontaneous moment of silence at the only monument to his memory we had so far.

I thought I would never forget him, but my memories have lost all movement; they've frozen into the photographed scenes on our outings: the three of us marching across a gravel path up to a placard or a panoramic view, my father leading the way with slight limp, and Gertrude and I, hand in hand, following. The memories have become generalized, and my time with him is now but one long excursion, during most of which I am sitting behind him in the car staring out the window, lost in my own thoughts.

He worked too much, but he was very dependable. My mother adored him. How she would hang on him. They often talked about how "when work slows down" we would move out of the city, and my father planned to write a book on mining history. Some of our outings were probably part of his research, I realized later.

And then one day he didn't come home from work.

His death intensified Gertrude's tendency to be busy. She felt she needed to *do something*. Volunteerism in general rose after 9/11, for a while anyway, and people got to working and hoping for each other, helping each other. Then slowly that withered away, and only the killing of one particular kind of fundamentalist continued to be inspired by the attack. Fear has more stamina than hope.

Chapter Four
Gluttony

Fatten the corporations, starve the intellectuals,
suckle the armies, and dry-nurse the land.
—Hamlet, after Pope

January 2003 – May 2004. When Gertrude and I moved to Amenia, she found a dying little hamlet in need of her attention. A vanquished hero on the field, Amenia had been, at one time, a wellspring of social good. During the Depression, the NAACP had its beginnings here, with a meeting among radical hopeful leaders that would shape the entire civil rights movement. Right here in Amenia, it's hard to believe. There are good people here in town whose proud fathers and mothers would have known about it firsthand. Gertrude supposed, mistakenly, that there breathed in Amenia a natural spirit for change and constant improvement. But the ghost of W. E. B. Du Bois moved not in the streets of Amenia, and must have confined itself to the outskirts of town, in the stately stone halls of Troutbeck, at which the meetings had taken place. The town center lacked a bronze statue of that inspiring man, and presented instead a monument to its own war-fallen sons.

Although officially change of any kind was not welcome in Amenia, it had been undergoing a slow and deadly transformation ever since the world wars. With this creeping kind of change, everything irresistibly flows downhill, and the lowest common denominator weighs down the weary feet of progress.

Gertrude had the idealistic notion that I would attend the public school, as a sacrificial offering to the noble idea of free and equal education for all. Public education for me had been out of the question in Brooklyn, but that's different, she said.

"Put him in day school where the *good* families put their kids," Polonius kept pleading.

But Gertrude would have none of it. A liberal education is the cure-all. The good John Adams said as much. In theory Gertrude and Adams were unquestionably right, but what kind of education? Our vast unwieldy public cannot agree on the basic assumption about what education is for, much less how to go about it. Is it to gain marketable skills? Or happiness? Is it to prepare one to earn money, in order to contribute to the system rather than take from it? Or is it to prepare one for the voting booth? Gertrude assumed the latter. Therein lay her problem. I had 70K in capital gains to live on per year and a mortgage-free estate to inherit. The other children had other fates to consider.

There were no indications that critical thinking skills were encouraged within the walls of the Webutuck district schools. Albeit well-intended, federal pressure on the district had, over the years, done what top-down control does, producing an industrial agricrop of students, whose natural abilities to learn and ask questions had been systematically replaced by reflex bigotry and fear of the unfamiliar. Undeterred by these signals, my mother bravely decided that a school is what you make of it, and she determined she would help transform the barely literate locals into book-loving souls, who would master Euclid in elementary school and appreciate Poincaré before graduation. I suspect she had some impossibly vague romantic notion about rural people having a natural intelligence derived from their intimate interrelations with the seasons and crops. She didn't know the history of the town yet, and she mistakenly assumed the students were gentlemen farmers' sons and daughters. The many farms that covered the district were, it turns out, owned by a single company whose headquarters were in Brussels, and they grew corn strictly for high fructose corn syrup and ethanol.

In the city I had been at a good Montessori with other normal-sized children. I was not prepared for what I met on my first day at Webutuck Elementary. Picture me waiting in line in the school cafeteria: my thin frame even thinner then, hair lying like a crow's wing across one eye, mouth open in shock. I still can recall with cinematic clarity the monochromatic meal, the beige tray on which a "pancake" wrapped in cellophane lay next to several oozy ounces of maple-flavored corn syrup, smiley fries, and a sealed plastic cup of heavily sweetened apple sauce. An unhappy, obese lunch lady wearing a sleeveless smock handed me a lukewarm chocolate milk carton, which had come all the way from Texas to the former home of Borden. The flesh of her bare upper arm, twice that of a ham hock, shook like gelatin.

Incredulous, still open-mouthed, I sought a seat in the crowded cafeteria, glancing around at the fifty or so outrageously obese students and teachers who were squeezed in around the tables, rear ends spilling over the attached mushroom stools. At an otherwise empty table a dark, very thin and tiny Indian girl sat alone eating carrots. I warily sat at the far end of her table and she smiled sarcastically, baring a set of impossibly perfect bright white teeth. Two boys plumped down on either side of me.

"I'm Guildenstern."

"I'm Rosencrantz."

"So you're the new kid."

"I'm Hamlet," I said offering my hand to Rosencrantz, who seemed not to notice. I tried Guildenstern, who likewise seemed not to know what to do with a proffered hand. Awkwardly I withdrew my offer and wiped my hand on my jeans.

They were the bullies—the sardonic smiles, the intense stares—but they were the only two children I had met so far who made eye contact. That was something. The rest shuffled to and fro with downcast eyes like psych center inmates. In general, if you said hello to parents or children in the school district they reacted with a mixture of fright and indignation, and they gave you a good dose of derisive laughter if you introduced yourself. 'What are you getting so high and mighty about?' was the suggested look. Apparently any kind of polite formality was considered uppity.

The Webutuckians saw so little change, and what they did see—huge equestrian estates going up in the hills around them—they did not like. A new student might insult them in a thousand different ways just by being different, for being different meant you did not approve of the way they did things. If one wanted to fit in in the Webutuck district, one just had to buckle down and reproduce here for a generation or two.

"Are you the welcoming committee then?" I asked, sighing.

"I think I've seen you around," said Rosencrantz. "You a weekender gone feral?"

"Feral, that's good. No, not a weekender."

"I give him three months before Principal Gates expels him."

I was surprised by the prediction.

Three months later, I was in the principal's office wearing the same surprised expression. A cluttered yard of Formica desk, with a false walnut grain, separated me and Mr. Gates as he explained, "Hamlet, we take pride in our district's name. 'Webutuck' derives from the native group that farmed this land in the infancy of this county." Mr. Gates was in his fifties with a bottlebrush grey mustache. That day he was wearing a sports jacket and khaki slacks, in honor of dress-down Friday, in a school where few boys owned collared shirts or leather shoes, and whose idea of "dress up," for say a wedding or a funeral, might be wearing a blank T-shirt instead of one with a colorful video-game advertisement.

"I know. I'm sorry. It's just that I can't resist a pun. Let's call it a Shakespearean impulse."

He didn't seem to want to call it that.

The janitor had reported a Sharpie tag on the bathroom wall. Apparently, Mr. Gates didn't consider for a second that any other of the boys might have done it. I was the first and only suspect. "You know, everyone seems so unhappy." I went on, trying to sound really concerned, "They can't look at you in the eye."

Mr. Gates, who had been staring at his desk, glanced up.

"Pardon the frankness Sir, but *webefucked*. The kids here haven't got a chance. You can see that starting by first grade when rotundity starts to set in. You're obviously not from around here. Your arms hang at right angles to the floor." I thought Mr. Gates was fighting back the temptation to be impressed with my rhetorical skill. I went on confidently, "By fifth grade, Mr. Gates, the kids can't see their feet. They haven't a chance. They're so sugared up from the federal breakfast and lunch program, I don't believe they can think." The last observation I had been able to make thanks to the familiarity I had with nutrition policies from the many meetings to which Gertrude had dragged me. "And the pyramid. Really *that much* bread?" I said parroting Gertrude. "Heavy on the milk and meats too, for god's sake. Industrial agriculture supported at the expense of children's health and the economic viability of small vegetable farms?" I paused, thinking I had begun to win him over. "The grammatical error is the clever part, don't you think? Totally supports the content."

I was expelled for the remaining month of the school year. "We be" come to think of it, as I left Mr. Gates's office, isn't the right regional dialect. Must do better next time.

In that month of exile, I caught up on all the reading I had missed in the previous months in school. The following September, Gertrude didn't bother to put me back in school, or rather, on the first day of the school year, she looked at the clock and said, "Hamlet, come on. Put down that book and get on the school bus." I was at a leisurely breakfast, enjoying a vegetable omelet that I had made myself after collecting the eggs. I looked up from my book, some big fat history, blinked rapidly three times and went on reading.

Gertrude wasn't a wage earner and there were plenty of farm chores to keep me busy, so it was pointless, we realized, for me to go to school, if the objective was to receive an education. (Although I was a little sad to leave my two friends, R & G, of whom I had grown fond, in a weird way.)

The *de facto* motto of Webutuck was, "Mediocrity: it's the best." I remember the first time I had visited the school library I had thought I might pick up some Twain, and went toward the high school section. The librarian, doing his best Michael Palin impersonation, waved his arms, "Stop that. Stop that," and steered me toward an "age appropriate" book derived from the latest TV adventure series. He had a "five finger" rule: count five unknown words on the first five pages and the book is too difficult. (*Huckleberry Finn* waits to be read in Webutuck.)

In English class, we neither read nor wrote. I was taught all the names of things that I already knew by feel, in order to prepare me for filling in bubbles on standardized tests. The other children, if they are lucky, will be able to remember for a month or two how to identify a "simile" from a list, but may never have a favorite one from *Romeo and Juliet*. For our creative writing assignments, i.e. filling in blanks, we were urged not to use difficult words because we might use them out of context or misspell them. Hippopotomonstrosesquippedaliophobia came to mind. (Fun fact: 20 percent of Webutuck parents do have misspellings in their tattoos.)

During my short stay in the district, I had observed that teacher autonomy, as little as it was suffered, still held out some promise for the students. Once I had gotten a detention for reading in class while I was supposed to be doing a workbook exercise. During that hour after school, my teacher revealed to me that she actually *liked* literature, and we spent the hour chitchatting about books. She was near retirement; a necklace of half glasses lay on her pneumatic breast. Her red curly hair went at all angles. She told me that she had "gone rogue," defying the administration. She said I would no longer have to do the curriculum. Instead, I would be allowed to read and write as I pleased the entire class hour. Unfortunately, she suddenly disappeared one day, and a company man replaced her.

Her replacement enforced the standardized curriculum with a vengeance. All of us had to memorize the same 175 facts for the grade. We were not authorized to do independent study or to memorize a fact that wasn't on the approved list. And we were not allowed to misspell.

"How the hell are we ever going to learn anything if we don't make mistakes?" I asked when the new teacher finally called on me. That resulted in my first of dozens of visits to Gates.

Gertrude had not managed to do any better than I that experimental year. While I was busy making enemies among my classmates and school administrators, Gertrude worked on the parents and the school board. Upon leaving the school, I joked to Mr. Gates, "If you see us tarred and feathered by the side of the road, give us a lift out of town." He didn't laugh.

In her dealings with the district, Gertrude had thought it made sense to start with basic health concerns before moving on to academic issues. She's lucky she never got that far. They thought she was radical for wanting to put black beans or vegetable soup on the menu. She never got the chance to try to push her educational immersion philosophy, allowing not a whit of dumbing down, which, she said, was like pruning too soon; it stunts growth. She claimed that children should be *encouraged* to be confused for significant periods of time. She claimed childhood is all about the blissful time in which being right and precise is not as important as getting a feel for a whole context with all the relevant as well as irrelevant detail. Fills the brain out, she'd say. Makes one open-minded. Being not quite right about a lot of things is better than knowing one or two things for sure, when you're a kid.

She brought me along to her first meeting in the Webutuck district (she brought me to most of them). In the fall of 2003, the federal government charged all schools with putting together a "Wellness Plan" in order to stimulate consumer spending in a new way and to pretend to address the childhood obesity crisis that was spreading across the country like plague in a shantytown. In January she read about the meeting in the paper, marked it on her calendar, gathered together all the nutrition data she had amassed over her years as SuperMom and drove to the school.

I carried her files for her as we walked across the parking lot. (I love my mother dearly, you see, always will.) The single-storey windowless campus sprawled over acres of former cow pastures, far from the villages it served. The new construction had replaced a stately ʰnineteenth century brick building in town, which moldered now in abandon. The new school buildings had been constructed in the seventies during a brief population boom and now served a student body one-third the capacity. Done in the then-fashionable warehouse style, the school had floors of polished concrete and walls of cinderblock with gobbed-on grey paint. The classrooms were without a single aesthetic element: nothing of beauty, not a beveled edge, mitered corner, cornice, or square foot of worn wood grain. It was all dreadfully systematic and discouraging. The allusion to prison could not be lost on the students.

I had already adjusted to the size-ratio thing, having attended school for a couple of weeks, but Gertrude was not prepared for what she saw when she entered the cafeteria where the meeting was to be held. Sitting on one side of a long table was a sort of stranded elephant seal version of the Last Supper, presumably the "wellness" committee.

The lunch lady was there, looking sleepy and shy. Light brown hair pulled back into a tiny cinnamon bun, she had a stack of files laid out in front of her. Her head was but a tiny planet stuck upon the Betelgeuse of her body. Somewhere inside all that flesh was a very petite woman. She had relatively short arms, a bit like a bloated tick. She had to squeeze her breasts together with her forearms in order to bring her hands close enough together to open a file.

Gertrude had asked me to take notes for the meeting and set me up at the far corner of the table. She took a seat opposite the others. Awkward silence passed during which they appeared to be waiting for something. Gertrude nervously suggested they all go around the table and introduce themselves. They shot each other glances and shifted in their seats. *She acts like she don't know who we are!* They already knew exactly who she was, where she lived, and why she was there. There was no reason to introduce themselves to one another; they all had grown up together, some of them were cousins, all of them had in-laws or step-kin in common.

"I'm Gertrude," she began. "That's my son, Hamlet. He's in sixth grade now."

I raised my hand, but they ignored me.

Reluctantly they began to give up their names. The lunch lady in her sleeveless smock was Kimmie Hogg (I'm not making this up), who, it appeared, was not just in charge of serving but also meal planning. The exercise and fitness expert, Coach Redman, was a man in his fifties with a raw hamburger face, wearing Smurf white gym shoes, a collared knit shirt, and kelly green polyester coach slacks. His way-past-term beer belly threw a shadow over spindly legs. He was going to keel over with heart failure any minute. To his left was Booz (his actual Dutch family name on his birth certificate) Hamilton, who owned a liquor store. He had no interest in school affairs and no particular expertise to offer. He attended meetings strictly for the social life. He had a habit of wearing blue jumpsuits that zippered down the front. A belt did not exist that was the length of his equator. The others were local pillars of the community: Tom Statfor, grocery store manager, and Ed Jefferson, hardware store owner and volunteer fireman—who was definitely not fitting through the average bedroom window. They all liked to serve on committees (some were also on the school or town board) for the purposes of keeping the school budget under control and taxes low. Of the gang of six only two, Kimmie and Ed, had a child in the school system. None of them had gone to college. All were Webutuck alumni.

Gertrude began by complimenting the new salad bar in the cafeteria, even though I had complained to her about the red-tinged, nutrient-free iceberg lettuce and fat-free ranch dressing with its modified food starch substituting for healthy olive oil. The committee members would later remember that she had begun by declaring Kimmie "too fat to know anything." But that was not Gertrude: often to her detriment, she tended to give people the benefit of the doubt. It was like Gertrude to suppose that Kimmie might have been far fatter once, had lost dozens of pounds, and was now an expert on Type 2, and that's what qualified her for the job. Or perhaps she supposed Kimmie was victim of her own culinary skills, a superb bread maker or cake baker or concoctor of gravies and rich sauces. (Not.) Throughout her dealings with the committee, Gertrude would be careful never to so much as mention "fat" or "obese" or even "chunky" when talking about peanut butter. Surrendering expediency to tact, after complimenting the wilted lettuce bar, Gertrude began her critique by making a modest suggestion to remove the least nutritional item on the menu and replace it with something healthy and cost-effective.

"The pancakes have got to go," I clarified from my corner.

During Gertrude's lecture, Kimmie had been listening with heavy lids and lips parted, glistening wet. Her breathing was deeply rhythmic, chest heaving slowly up and down, as if she were napping. Upon hearing my words, she objected dreamily, "That's one of our most popular items."

"Pancakes for lunch twice a week?" barked Gertrude. "I don't suppose they're *whole* wheat!"

Kimmie looked uncertain and hurt. Self-reproving Gertrude apologized for her tone.

I could see Kimmie thinking; the neglected gears in her brain squealed and lurched. The product of this cognition we would later see in the new menus she had printed the following week. They would proudly and defensively claim now to offer *wheat* rolls, and *wheat* breaded fishsticks, *wheat* bread, *wheat* pancakes, and *wheat* hot dog buns, where before the grain specification had not been included.

Coach Redman rose, rearranging his gut over his belt and explained, very kindly, "You're not from around here, so you don't know the history." Whenever any of the locals addressed us, they usually prefaced their remarks this way. "A lot of consideration went into the pancakes. You see, since the pancakes are 'yam-flavored' pancakes, they satisfy both the federal 'vegetable' requirement and the 'bread' requirement. So as long as we get the kid to take a chocolate milk too, the school is guaranteed federal reimbursement for that meal." As he sat back down he added, "That pancake is going nowhere."

"Some kids don't eat at all. This may be their one meal of the day," Booz put in. "My nephew is on medication for hyperactivity," he ruminated on a wad of something as he paused, "and he is not eating any vegetables. If you don't have something good on the menu, that kid is not going to eat. Can't have children going hungry."

"Anyone think of discontinuing the medication?" offered Gertrude.

"You can always offer a health food option, but kids need to have *choice*," said the coach, and as he found that last word he seemed surprised at his own cleverness, having hit upon just the right word to appeal to the likes of Gertrude.

I raised my hand and asked, "I'm sorry Coach, but is that two healthy choices like soup or salad? Or one unhealthy and one healthy, like cake or salad?"

He stared back at me blankly as if I were a barnyard animal that had just spoken.

"He's taking notes for me," Gertrude explained. "It's okay Hamlet."

Gertrude and I had done this kind of thing together before. We had a routine.

"Can the children have the option of water at lunch instead of sweetened milk?" Gertrude had mastered her emotions and spoke without frustration. I was reminded of the way she had handled my childhood tantrums, voice melodic, inquisitive, nonthreatening.

But now the coach was losing patience and the others were clearly bored. "I just told you, without a milk sale, the lunchroom would lose its government subsidy."

"I see your point," Gertrude went on bravely, "but—" she faltered, realizing she had used a negative word, then regaining form, she continued "—and we also know that caloric liquids are a leading cause of ob—weight gain. When you're thirsty your body requires water for hydration."

"There're water fountains in the hall."

"And we could put pitchers on the tables," replied Gertrude.

"We don't have any pitch—"

Gertrude broke in, "I'll pick up a dozen and donate them to the school."

Booz smirked while the other faces continued to frown. "That's very generous of you, but we can't do water pitchers," Booz said. "The insurance costs would be sky high. There will be too many spills. Someone could slip."

"I'm sure you have spills sometimes?"

"But not like water spills," said Kimmie.

"No not like big water spills," agreed the coach. "The school business manager is never going to let *that* one fly."

I recorded in my notes, "Serving water impossible, inconceivable."

Gertrude went cheerfully on, "Soups are very healthy and cost-effective—"

"High school kids don't eat soup," Coach Redman interrupted.

Gertrude ignored him, "You can make soups out of leftovers."

"Mystery soup!" said Booz. They all laughed until they coughed. Finally, wiping a tear from his eye—pure histrionics—Booz said, "Nah, seriously, Kimmie. How about the lady's suggestion?" stifling more laughter.

Kimmie explained, in her meek, exhausted way, that the kitchen was located fifty yards from the actual lunchroom, and they couldn't transport the soup because it tended to spill. "It slops over on the way."

"Do you use lids?" asked Gertrude.

"Yeah, but they never fit right," she answered, despairing, her small voice trailing off.

"Soup is no good when it's hot out," said Coach Redman.

The five others agreed, "Oh, yeah, good point."

I wrote down, "Soup opposed six to one."

"Brown rice and beans," Gertrude suggested next. "Our student body is currently 13 percent Hispanic," she added, looking at her file.

They shot each other indignant glances, as if they had just been insulted. No one replied. Booz folded his arms on his chest and leaned back a little.

I wrote, "*Arroz y frijoles, no es apropiado.*"

As the meeting went on, Gertrude tried to pin down exactly what the procedures were for ordering the food. The group was evasive, saying only: Carlyle would know that; you should ask Carlyle.

Finally, about an hour into the meeting, a dark-haired man in an unbuttoned double-breasted suit entered the room, heaving his enormous body left then right, left, right, walking himself across the floor as if he were a refrigerator. He lowered himself down next to Kimmie and took her palm in his hand and patted it. This was Carlyle Hogg, the school board president.

Booz got up, offering Hogg a wooden gavel, which he had drawn from his coat pocket. Frowning, Hogg gestured that would not be necessary. The others gazed at him with rapture as he got himself settled in his seat, smiling pleasantly. Fried shrimp and cigarette smoke odor wafted from the folds of his jacket.

Hogg had served a dozen years in the army. The town hero was an explosives expert whose job it was, I suppose, to disarm bombs and mines. ("Uh, let's get Hogg to do it.") The corporeal corporal had been back from Afghanistan a year—already tripling his desert weight on Kimmie's food.

"Sorry I'm late. Train delays." None of the others knew what it was like to suffer train delays. Extraordinary among locals, Hogg now commuted into the city for work in the counterterrorism business. Many of his friends had not been to the city ever in their lifetimes. "Didn't have time to change out of my monkey suit." The others obediently laughed.

Hogg's fans then begged him for updates on the "situation." He bewailed his bad fortune of having retired from the army just when they needed him most, allowing us to imagine that he would have been the one to disarm the WMDs. Hogg shook his head, "The whole damned region needs a good thrashing. If we don't do it, every Mohammed Al-Fortinbras in the world will be pestering us with demands to surrender those lands lost by their fathers, with all bonds of law." (That's what I have down in my notes. I may have embellished.)

Kimmie said she did not like to hear talk about her husband leaving her again for the Middle East. Carlyle had worn a uniform at their wedding, which had taken place right after high school, and she wanted him all to herself now. I imagined her long lonely years on the sofa in front of CNN, with a can of Pringles in her lap.

Meanwhile, Gertrude was studying a chocolate milk carton. "A single serving of this milk contains *three times* the USDA recommended daily amount of sugar, and it's HFCS, high fructose corn syrup!"

"High fruit-o wha?" chuckled Hogg. The others mimicked.

Gertrude smiled vaguely. "Three times the amount," she repeated simply.

"Everything in moderation," Hogg wisely replied.

I wrote down, "Excess in moderation okay."

"What about plain milk?"

"The state makes us sell nonfat. The kids won't take it. Tastes like piss," said Booz.

On the way home, Carlyle and Kimmie were in the car ahead of ours. We saw them turn off into their driveway, and we noticed on the porch of their peeling Victorian, amid broken rocking chairs and plastic toys, was a spare extra-capacity upright refrigerator.

For months the committee accomplished nothing; mainly they spent the time criticizing Gertrude's "style" and "approach," which they considered "negative." The important thing, they kept reiterating, was to respect each other's opinions and to provide "choices." To this end, Kimmie Hogg brought in some PepsiCo vending machines that sold *organic* snack foods, like organic potato chips, organic toaster pies, and organic ice cream sandwiches. Gertrude admitted this wasn't quite what she'd had in mind. The fireman, who I cannot recall having said a word through the three or four meetings I had attended, and who had not yet appeared in my notes, at last could take no more. "I have to say, I haven't spoke up at meetings, mainly because of a certain person who seemed to feel the need to pick apart every word of what people say. Basically Kimmie was just trying to put something out there that people might enjoy. If you don't want your child to eat pancakes or Pop-Tarts, then pack a lunch for him. Parents don't need to be made to feel bad about the choices they give their children."

The grocery store manager was also inspired to speak for the first time. "I realize everyone has a right to express their opinion, but just because you have a right don't mean you should. This is supposed to be a group where we help each other, not tear each other down." As he sat down he mumbled, "Have a blessed day."

"Thank you Ed, Tom. That's really helpful," said Gertrude. "Since this is a school, we should be teaching the kids how to make healthy choices. What's *your* favorite healthy food?"

"I guess it would be . . . Diet Coke?" said Ed as if he were on a game show offering the $10,000 answer. If only I had a "wrong" buzzer.

"Granola bars are all right," said Tom.

"Okay. Granola bars are *whole-grain* cookies, that's something," said Gertrude. "But if you ate a handful of nuts instead, you'd get some essential oils and tryptophan, a precursor of serotonin—"

Hogg's gavel sounded, and the meeting was brought to an end.

As rumors about the troublesome newcomer started going around town, it became awkward to visit the grocery store. When Gertrude's back was turned, I would see heads leaning together, whisperings insults, and nodding in our direction. It was especially embarrassing to run into Kimmie at Foodtown. Goody Two-Shoes Gertrude's cart contained only fresh produce. "Hi Kimmie. How are you? Getting a little shopping in before the holiday?" While she spoke Gertrude would put her body in front of her cart to keep Kimmie from seeing its exemplary contents, and she tried hard to avert her gaze from Kimmie's cart packed with neon boxes.

Every once in a while Gertrude found some support from old timers, people whose last names echoed street signs and the oldest tombstones in the graveyard along Route 343. Once in the foreign foods section, a white bearded sage whispered in Gertrude's ear, "Facts don't matter. Once you understand that you will get on better." Then he disappeared.

Inspired by the man's encouragement, Gertrude kept at it. She contacted farm cooperatives nearby and planned a farm-to-school program. She researched the cost of a milk dispenser so that they could sell plain local milk at a price comparable to that of the industrial dairies far away. She found a swine farmer who was eager to purchase all the cafeteria food wastes (though he was somewhat concerned about the possible low quality of school food, so she had to promise him the menu would include food fit for swine). She shot off dozens of e-mails to other committee members describing the work she had done and urging them to read the "interesting" research she had found about the ill effects of processed foods. She suggested a "Bikes For Transportation Not Just Recreation" fund-raising campaign to connect the rail trail bike path to the school, which, she calculated, would save tens of thousands in bus service expenses. (She would also have the remaining diesel buses run on used cooking oil.)

The meetings grew smaller and were frequently postponed without explanation. After a while, Gertrude and I were sometimes the only ones who showed up at the scheduled meetings. We would sit in the cafeteria, she with her research and her pamphlets, I with my notebook, which was now full of doodles, waiting for the others to arrive.

Coach Redman was about the only one who showed up with any regularity. "I guess we can't get started until we have a quorum." He mostly avoided wellness committee topics and stuck to school sports instead. In former days, he liked to remember, Webutuck was almost best in state. "All the parents came to all the games. Now we are lucky if the players show up. We've lost every game, every year, for five years now. I try to stay positive, you know, and encourage the kids, because they do a real fine job."

"Mr. Redman, did you see the link I sent about the new community-supported agriculture group? If we loan them use of our kitchen during the summer, we can get free canned vegetables."

"Call me Coach," he admonished her gently. He had a crush on her. "Are those hippies even certified by the USDA?"

When she told him about the school garden she was planning, he offered to get his friend at AllChem to donate bags of fertilizer.

But then one weekend Coach Redman had a massive coronary and died midweek, leaving Gertrude completely without a committee. Now no one answered her e-mails. No one came.

While Gertrude still imagined bright smiling farmers unloading bushels of healthy greens at the school loading docks, trucks from Albany warehouses continued to rattle down Route 22, filled with processed heat-and-eat "chicken" fingers and cellophane-wrapped, crustless "peanut" butter and "grape" jelly sandwiches, whose label made no mention of peanuts or grapes (instead there was palm oil and HFCS).

Finally, months later, after a few hours poring over the school board minutes archived online, I discovered that the certified school nutritionist had been fired about the time that Hogg had returned home from the "war" and became school board president. I showed Gertrude how some personnel shuffling had occurred, catapulting Kimmie (if you can imagine that metaphor) from cook assistant into the nutritionist's position, for which she lacked all qualifications. Gertrude's heart melted a little when she noted that although Kimmie's new position gave her an increase in salary, her pay was still miserably low.

Gertrude prepared a careful report and included recommendations for removal of Hogg from the school board, and handing off responsibility for nutrition guidelines to the wellness committee, demoting Kimmie (without a pay cut) to the position of cook—although "can opener" might have been more precise since nothing raw ever entered the premises (food safety laws); no vegetables were diced; no ingredients mixed.

Gertrude said that when she arrived at the principal's office to hand in her report, a suited man stood ominously behind Mr. Gates. His attire had a correctness about it that distinguished him from the few others in town who wore suits—the banker, Mr. Gates himself, a few of the male teachers. He was Mr. Cretan, the district's attorney sent down from Albany. Mr. Gates, acting under orders no doubt, was perfectly quiet throughout the entire meeting. Mr. Cretan promised, "We'll get back to you" and was never heard from again.

I was expelled a few days after Gertrude submitted the report. Fortunately, in our exile, Gertrude and I soon discovered there was another side to Amenia, and we had only so far been acquainted with the squalid results of the '70s boom—the factory-style school, the warehouse supermarket and strip mall—all disconnected from the old Amenia hamlet area, which we had completely overlooked. At the foot of DeLaVergne Hill, where the single crossroads of Amenia lay, there was a stately stone bank on the corner, across the street five or six antique stores, a perfectly quaint post office, the town justice with shingle outside and a small red brick "free library" established pre-Civil War. The hamlet was actually on its way up again after decades of decay. Two cafés opened; newly renovated, their '70s false fronts had been removed, revealing old Victorian columns that had been hidden in undeserved shame for thirty years.

The locals that we had come to know through the school refused to patronize these charming shops and cafés, which were to them but phony façades put on for the citiots going through town on their way to the Berkshires. Instead, they patronized the strip mall stores, the pizza place or Chinese food restaurant next to the supermarket, but they really longed for an Applebees, at which they could order pizza or Chinese food. These two Amenias existed side by side like parallel universes that denied the existence of the other.

After spending an arcadian summer enjoying this alter-Amenia, Gertrude got a letter from Mr. Gates around October saying that she needed to come in and explain why I hadn't come back to school yet, and if she planned to "homeschool," there were forms for us to fill out.

We drove up Route 22 to the school compound sitting alone on its windy hill. Some weeks previously, after a parent in a neighboring school district had taken an administrator hostage (parent shot, student expelled), the Webutuck district had responded with a lockdown procedure of its own. All parents, who had not been welcome on school grounds before, were now forbidden to enter without passing by Charon, the secretary who hated everyone and always forgot your name. "Why are you here?" she barked at Gertrude through the intercom at the entrance.

"I'm here to see Mr. Gates. It's Gertrude, Charon."

She buzzed, and we were allowed in. Charon leered at Gertrude for a full minute and then directed a big brown-tooth smile at me. "Hello Hamlet. How have you been? Would you like some candy?" She pointed to the crystal dish on her desk filled with super-sized Mars bars. I looked at Gertrude and blinked three times.

"I just brushed," I said finally.

"Go on in," she mumbled.

Mr. Gates had put on weight and was sweating a little. After shaking both our hands he sat behind his desk with a sigh. "Rough couple of weeks."

"I'm sure it was horrible," said Gertrude.

"Pretty scary stuff. But no one was hurt; that's all that matters," said Mr. Gates, then remembering, "Except for the dad."

"What was the complaint? I mean, what set him off?" I asked.

"Oh, they all claim their kids are getting too much homework and their grades are too low."

Above Mr. Gates's head, "1,097.6" was affixed to the wall. It was made out of craft-store wood numbers, hand painted in the school color, kelly green. He noticed that Gertrude was looking at it.

"That number," he said, "represents the number of different educational experiences that the Webutuck children will have as they pass through the district from Pre-K to twelfth grade." He paused. "But you're leaving the district —."

"No, please go on."

"Currently every one of the twenty-four point five children in each class gets a slightly different curriculum from his or her teacher, and there are three point two teachers per grade, making the total number of educational experiences for one grade level seventy-eight point four. By the time one of our seventy-eight point four students per grade graduates from Webutuck he or she may have had any one of the one thousand ninety-seven point six different educational experiences offered here. It is my goal to reduce that number to *one*," he said holding up a fat finger. "Next year, the curriculum committee will decide upon all assignments in class and for homework and every student will be expected to do the same units. We're going to get those test scores up to where they should be, so that our graduates can achieve their highest earning potential."

"One educational experience?" asked Gertrude, voice cracking.

He nodded confidently.

"What if you accidentally pick the wrong one?" I asked. "Wouldn't it be better to spread the risk with a variety of approaches?"

"What do you mean, *picked the wrong one?*" Mr. Gates replied, exasperated. "The curriculum committee will decide exactly what is needed based on federal and state requirements. Every child in America deserves the best education we can give them. No excuses. Districts all over the country are doing this. If New York increased its college attainment rate by just 1 percent—from 33.8 to 34.8 percent —the state would capture a $17.5 billion talent dividend."

"Is your degree an MBA?" Gertrude asked.

"No." He looked confused. He signed the paperwork to be finally rid of Gertrude and me.

Months later, nearing the end of the school year, the local paper announced the district had finally completed a Wellness Plan. It was called, "Health Comes in All Sizes." The school board was celebrating the occasion by hosting an all-you-can-eat breakfast in the school cafeteria. Curious, we decided to go.

Rosencrantz was winning the sausage-eating contest when we arrived. He was ahead of Guildenstern by two pounds. It was apparent both had planned for the event, wearing exercise pants with elastic waistbands. The eating contest custom at Webutuck was more honour'd if their breeches were not observed to breach. But their camouflage T-shirts could not obscure the stains of the orgy that had gone on now for an hour.

Half the senior class wore army attire and would soon be shipping off to the Fertile Crescent between the Tigris and Euphrates, bringing Round-Up-Ready wheat to the unlucky inhabitants of those ancient civilizations that had first domesticated grains.

The black-booted and camouflaged valedictorian, Gazelle Humphreys, was taking the podium at the end of long rows of littered lunch tables—strewn with the lumps of brown foodstuff and ooze-coated Styrofoam plates that were the remains of their feast. Gazelle was to make a speech based on her senior research project, which had been the inspiration for the new Wellness Plan. Carlyle Hogg, who was wearing desert fatigues which he must have had custom-made out of his old tent, passed out copies to the eager and attentive audience, softly grunting as he leaned across the rows of shoulders. Gertrude and I shared a copy. The two hundred pound senior's five-page report displayed the highest achievements of district essay writing. The footnotes, abjectly insisting upon the credibility of the research, pointed to three Wikipedia entries, a mainstream newspaper OpEd, a brochure from a celebrity eating disorders clinic, and footnotes that referred to other footnotes—whose content had been transformed along the way like a message in the game telephone. The argument went this way: when a teacher giving a nutrition lesson says some foods are "good" and others "bad," children internalize the "bad" label. Such indoctrination is the leading cause of anorexia. The terrifying statistics of anorexia were enumerated. Gazelle's closing lines were moving, "You've got to enjoy life, not give up McDonald's," and then she added, raising her operatic voice, "It's a quality of life issue."

The approving crowd roared. Gertrude, whose face was blank, had failed to imagine that obesity could be a lifestyle choice. She looked at her lap. It had never occurred to her. She had thought that they only needed guidance. She was humbled. She turned to look at me. My jaw was dropped in disbelief. But she raised a hand of benediction. Who was she to force her values on them?

It was clear that Gertrude's healthy food campaign was more than finished. But Gazelle wasn't done yet. The crowd wanted more—because behind it all, behind all the criticism of "fat" people and "junk" food, what Gertrude had been after was their happiness, their freedoms, their beliefs and their values. Webutuck did not need Gertrude's hoity-toity ideas, her good-for-nothing philosophizing that was of no use in the global marketplace where consumption is the measure of success. They did not need her elitist son who didn't even have a favorite team and thought he was too good for "Call of Duty" (at this they all laughed, how true!). Their own level-ninety sons were prepared for the hi-tech future of this country.

All at once they raised their fists. Democratic capitalism has spoken, and the best now has obliterated all the rest. One farm, one nation, undereducated, indivisible, with security and convenience for all.

These Webutuck parents would never give up their food-stamp-and-Medicaid-supplemented-part-time service jobs to go back to digging in dirt like their hayseed ancestors. Didn't Gertrude understand that the biotech industry had made nature obsolete? The students and their families believed it was their patriotic duty to purchase heat-and-eat foods in support of military-style farming, whose tank-like tractors fought for their freedom in front of the flat screen.

Holly Burton, an orb-shaped parent, struggled to her tiny feet amid more cheering and pounding on the tables. "We have a right to teach our children what we want," Holly yelled, yellow ribbon pinned to her heaving breast. "No one is going to tell me I cannot give my Ariel a Pop-Tart. Mind your damned own business," she said directly to Gertrude. (Sitting next to her mom was enormous Ariel, with heavy lids and dull stare—metabolism ruined, damned to diabetes.) "This is America; we are free to choose."

Holly was right. Genetic propagandizing (which could legally be directed at citizens now) has subdued the biodiverse rout into a gentle majority monocrop. The unwanted grass and birds and bees have been beaten back with chemical warfare.

This was not just about the new Wellness Plan. This was Webutuck's day of victory, and they had a right to fatten on the spoils of war. What remained of their victims, the highly processed carcasses of the bovine POWs, traveled through the guts of Rosencrantz and Guildenstern and all the rest. And they were happy.

"This is America," the hoarse nation croaked.

As Gertrude and I ran for the door, the voices grew louder and louder, cheering for modified food starch and MSG, aspartame and Lunchables.

"GMO!" they shouted, "GMO!"

Chapter Five
Forget-me-not Ophelia

May 2003 - December 2003. After I was expelled, Rosencrantz and Guildenstern came over on R's four-wheeler after their school day ended or on weekends. While Gertrude watched us play through the window, R & G pulled the ladder away from my tree house trapping me inside, R threw a fastball into my nose, G planted stones on my bike paths. Once Gertrude witnessed the beheading of Charles, my favorite rooster. They laughed loudly and creepily as he ran around headless while I pleaded, shedding hot tears.

Gertrude, in her so-polite-that-it-doesn't-make-sense way of speaking, "invited" them to not come over anymore, but she still worried that I needed more peer interaction than Pluto provided. Her solution was to call up old Polonius and arrange a playdate with little Ophelia. Polonius was eager to accommodate for reasons that were never quite clear to me; one suspects he was in love with Gertrude, but she obviously never entertained that idea, and let him go on acting as our personal assistant and counselor. They had sold their apartment on Park Avenue and were living in Millbrook full time now. Ophelia was, like me, in need of local friends.

I had met Ophelia a few times at her father's house, but had never really talked to her. I remember first seeing her barefoot in a lichen-colored slip of a dress, hugging a stack of botany books as she scurried across the tiled hallway to the stairs. Then I heard her footsteps above my head, a door slam and then blaring music. I wondered how she could study with the music so loud.

Ophelia was three years younger than I. As an eleven-year-old, very near twelve that summer, it was crucial that any age difference between my friends and me go the other way. I refused to participate in the playdate and rode off furiously on my bike. I was hiding in my tree house when her father's hearse-like Cadillac SUV lumbered down the drive. I saw her face in the backseat window. Her small pink palm was pressed against the glass, as if she were trapped inside. She looked up at the tree house where I was peering out the window. I thought our eyes met. Out of curiosity I slinked down the ladder and nonchalantly walked to the car where Polonius introduced me to his daughter with such awkwardness my heart wrenched for her. Smiling paternally and mussing her hair, he said, "This is Ophelia, her mother's favorite."

It was hard to believe Ophelia was eight. She *looked* six or seven, tiny in stature, baby-like teeth, smooth translucent skin, fine brown hair, head proportionally large, round eyes. But she acted older than my eleven years. She was an odd bird, like me, morose, furtive. Her hobby was biology and she was studying German because she claimed, "the best old books have never been translated." Now I wonder how she knew that since she wouldn't have been able to read them, but at the time I took it for gospel.

She collected dried flowers and practiced amateur taxidermy on all her beloved pets that had died. She wasn't very good at it (*yet*, she insisted) and some of her trophies were left odoriferously decaying in the garage.

"Are you into death?" I stupidly asked her that first afternoon.

She tossed her hair. "Obviously not, or I would be able to let go." (She had lost her mother when she was five.) Her first patient was a pet dusky parakeet that had broken its neck on a windowpane. She said it was hard skinning it, but the process helped you realize what dead really meant.

On her next visit she brought me a stuffed egret as a housewarming present for my tree house. We perched the bird in the eaves where he looked down upon us as we grasped each other's damp skin.

Her brother, Laertes, was ten years older than Ophelia. To me he was but a bright streak running by on his way to some impressive sports exhibition or award ceremony. Away at boarding school most of the time, a military academy in the tradition of his family, he would soon be off to Iraq. He had a plank-backed posture. He was the sort of boy that you read about in the paper, who, having led an exemplary life, suddenly ends it tragically by making some unfortunate—yet perfectly characteristic—choice. Straight teeth, muscular, tan, clean, he was not a superficial jock; there was something very old-fashioned about him, an unwavering dedication to order, duty and loyalty that made him unreal.

I envied his relationship with Ophelia. Healthy sibling contempt and rivalry was not there. In place of it was an intimacy I did not like. They wrote each other constantly.

Ophelia would receive many photos of her heroic brother wearing fatigues in dusty places, posing with armed-to-the-teeth nonchalance.

I never knew what had happened to their mother. A portrait of her—a painting not a photo—hanging in the dining room revealed that Ophelia took after her. How that boob Polonius managed to catch that beauty is a story I'd like to hear. She was an equestrian, and we can guess she broke her neck, like the parakeet.

Ophelia and I played together, really played like children should, in streams and thickets. We came home dirty and wet, carrying prized ferns and stones in our pockets or pieces of dead deer. I don't think any of the other local children explored the hills around the valley. It was an uncharted wilderness. We found old Native American and settler ruins that no one had seen in decades. Only the orange-vested hunters, who came in the fall, were rivals to our kingdom, but they had no interest in the romance of the woods or its history. Outside of a hunting cabin on Silo Ridge there were six or seven mattresses tossed out in a refuse pile. We assumed the hunters got so drunk sometimes they peed the bedding, which they had probably hauled up on four wheelers, and couldn't be bothered taking down again. Inside the cabin, I found a wood-burning stove, a set of thin pans and a can opener. Ophelia refused to use the cabin. We lay on pine needles instead at the top of the ridge near a clearing so that we could look down upon the valley. The cabin had a "pestilence," she claimed, and wouldn't even cross the threshold.

Our hikes through the wood were always done with the ultimate object of finding a convenient place to kiss. The moment we found a soft clean spot to lie down in, there was an awkward moment of silence, and then I usually made some apish attempt to wrestle with her, but then, when we were close enough, our lips would touch and I could put my cool hand inside her warm shirt. She would jump from my icy touch at first but eventually she would tolerate my hand on her belly, but never, of course, on her baby flat breasts. I looked into her seashell translucent ears and breathed in her warm sesame seed scent.

That summer was ending. We were lying on our favorite patch of grass on the southeast side of Silo Ridge, where the property owner had cleared trees to open up a panoramic view of Amenia. The trees had been chipped on site and clumps of mountain grass grew upon soft piles of wood mulch. To the west a stand of old white pines grew, and the wind blowing through the needles reminded Ophelia of the seashore. Down in the valley, the bright tin roof of my barn glinted in the afternoon sun surrounded by big cottonwood trees. There is something about being up high, being able to survey your property and feel the pride of ownership. I was still just a child, but the farm was mine as much as it was my mother's.

Ophelia did not have that same sense of security about her home. Polonius, throwback that he was, clearly intended to observe primogeniture and give his farm—lock, stock and barrel—to Laertes. There was some money that Ophelia's mother had left her in a trust, a fact Polonius liked to mention at awkward times. (Sometimes I wondered if Ophelia were really his daughter, but I never said this to her.) He was equally fond of reminding Ophelia that her horse stable and practice ring would eventually go to her brother, and she was at his mercy.

Dear Ophelia uncomplainingly accepted her fate. She could probably trust her brother to do the right thing.

Competent Laertes, in fact, seemed more like her father than grandfatherly Polonius, whose defining characteristics were feebleness and irrelevancy. I wanted to ask her if she could imagine herself being lady of the manor with me some day. Instead I asked, "What do you think you'll be doing in a dozen years?"

She bit her lip thinking for a long while then shrugged. "I don't know." She moved closer to me, took my arm and draped it over her shoulders. This seemed to me to be her way of saying that she was happy now with the way things were. "Do you remember the violets that you gave me in May?"

"I do."

"They were sweet but the perfume didn't last. I dried them."

"There will always be more violets, Ophelia. I will pick more for you every spring. You don't need to save them, unless you want to." We said nothing for a while. "The air was cooler this morning. Did you feel it? It crept into my bedroom window with bad news. Summer is ending, it said to me, and Ophelia won't come anymore. She'll be waiting at the bus stop in the dark with the other scholars while you are lying here cozy in your warm blankets."

"Why don't you go to Dutchess Day School with me?"

"I'd have to get up too early," I said, stretching my feet out in front of me and laying my head on my folded arms.

She lay down beside me. "Don't you have to get up early anyway?" She looked at me, a little cross-eyed at the short distance. I almost laughed but stopped myself before offending my sensitive mistress.

"The sheep don't get up until the sun does. Besides I like to take my time in the morning. I don't want to look at a clock. Ban all clocks. We should all use the sun and stars instead. Why does anybody have to be so punctual anyway? Don't we waste a lot of time leaving ourselves enough time to be on time? I can judge the hour within twenty minutes. That's good enough."

"We missed the train this morning," she pointed out.

We had planned to meet at the train station to go to the Museum of Natural History, but Gertrude and I had arrived late, and since trains run only every two hours, we couldn't make a proper day of it. "Well, that was my mom's fault. She couldn't find her keys."

"We'll try again," said Ophelia.

"Stay the night at our house tonight and we'll ride my bike to the train in the morning. I'll put you on the handle bars."

"Where will I sleep? Your bed is too small."

"We will camp out in the tree house or we can lie in the pasture with the sheep. Many a night have I lain in pastures beside my little flock, charting the changes in the night sky."

"You're crazy Hamlet."

"I am but mad north-north-west. When the wind is southerly, I know a hawk from a handsaw. I only seem mad because I'm a shepherd and we are out of style."

Ophelia didn't answer. The white pine tide was coming in. After a while, I blurted out, "I never want you to grow up. But you will. You will grow up and we will drift apart, but I'll be waiting for you. Ten years from today, no matter where you are in the world, promise me that you will come back here, to this spot when dark descends. I will be here waiting for you on August 27, 2013, at 9:18 p.m. If you don't come the sun will never rise again for me."

"How do you know when the sun will set ten years from now?"

"All shepherds know."

"Oh wait, it will get dark at the same time in ten years."

"Nothing is ever the same, really—except me. I won't change."

"Neither will I."

That night Polonius came to pick up Ophelia and would not agree to let her sleep over. "I'll describe the stars to you tomorrow," I said, as she entered into the deep dark depths of her father's car. I took my sleeping bag, determined to sleep under the sky for both of us, and found my flock resting under some wild honeysuckle about one hundred feet from the cottage. I unrolled my bedding in the open pasture. Pluto rose, in that funny way sheep have, rear-end first, and came to lie down beside me. I scratched him behind his curly horns and told him he was no substitute for Ophelia. As the sky darkened, slowly the other sheep left the cover of the honeysuckle and spread themselves out in the pasture a yard or two from each other, the little ones up against their moms. There was no moon, and the stars were very bright.

Amenia has almost no ground light at night, only the street lamps along the main arteries. Houselights in the interior fade to black around ten, and on cloudless nights, the Milky Way really begins to glow. That night I remembered, as I have a habit of doing, that once when I was just about three, I had been nursing at Gertrude's breast when we heard my father come in the door. I pulled away, and her milk went spraying out across the dark walnut headboard. "Look, it's the Milky Way," said my father, as he sat down on the bed after kissing his wife and son.

My parents had repeated that story to me often, so I don't know whether I actually remember it or remember the retellings, but I suppose it makes no difference. We only remember memories of rememberings.

"Look it's the Milky Way," I said aloud and cried myself awake for a long time before finally I slept.

The next morning I sat up and looked around. Dry patches of grass were dotted here and there where the sheep had slept in the now dew-covered pasture. The flock had gone to graze nearer to the cottage, all except young Pluto, who was a late riser like me. We must have been wakened by the same sound because he was also rousing himself. He looked about nervously bleating. The others answered immediately. He scrambled to his feet and ran to join them.

Ophelia, wearing a riding costume, followed by Polonius and Gertrude, was climbing the hill toward me. Gertrude, always perfectly attired at any hour, was dressed in a crisply ironed fitted shirt, lavender, canvas skirt and sensible leather boots. She was carrying a tray and Polonius had a rolled blanket tucked under his arm.

"I've already been out riding this morning while you slept," said Ophelia.

Polonius, with a dab of shaving cream stuck in a missed tuft of beard under his chin, spread the wool blanket out, and Gertrude set it with saucers for hot cocoa.

"What time is it? I'm frozen."

"Seven thirty," answered Ophelia brightly.

"Then you were up at dawn."

"I woke up at four and couldn't go back to sleep." Strands of chestnut hair escaped her ponytail. She looked sleepy.

"You need to get back in bed then. Come on and get inside with me. I need some warming up." I threw back the corner of my sleeping bag, and Ophelia shimmied in with me while Polonius smiled tolerantly.

"Your mother and I," he said, "are on our way to the county fair today to look at the livestock show."

"Want to come?" asked Gertrude, handing Ophelia hot cocoa but looking at me.

Polonius answered for her in the pompous manner he had of making everything sound like an announcement, "Ophelia is going to the fish and game for a taxidermy class."

"What, here in town or at the fair?" I asked.

"Here at the Amenia Hunter's Hut," answered Ophelia.

"You're sending her there, Polonius, among the brutes? I have friends that belong to the Hut. Ophelia isn't suited for that place. Rosencrantz and Guildenstern hunt for pleasure."

"I've already met them," said Ophelia, blowing on her cocoa with her deep mauve lips. "They're horrid. One is working on a bobcat and the other a brown eagle."

"I would think that would be against the law," said Gertrude, sipping.

"You know last year the police found a body on the property," I said to Polonius. "A human body."

"An unfortunate hunting accident no doubt," said Polonius stupidly.

"In a shallow grave. I should go with you Ophelia."

"But I was thinking of buying a cow," said Gertrude. "Don't you want to help me pick her out?"

I thought awhile. I couldn't really trust Polonius to help my mother make the right decision, but the thought of

Rosencrantz and Guildenstern playing pranks on Ophelia, teasing her, or flirting with her made me resolve: "I think I'll go with Ophelia."

"You're not a member."

"And you are? Of the Hut? Oh, Ophelia. They are the same bunch of hunters that piss all over those mattresses."

"What?" asked Gertrude.

I had not mentioned the hunting cabin to my mother.

"There is a cabin on Silo Ridge where we hike," said Ophelia.

"Trespassing?" asked Polonius.

"I suppose," said Ophelia indifferently.

Polonius shot Gertrude a look making her frown. In the end (after Gertrude told Polonius about R & G), we all went to the fair together to pick out the cow. Slow-gaited Polonius got lost in the crowd twice, and we spent so much time trying to find him, we got to the auction late and ended up bringing home a poor thin animal with a lame foot. On the long return ride, Ophelia and I sat together in the backseat, she in the jump seat in the middle, her head falling on my shoulder. Polonius peeked at us in the rearview mirror and my mother turned her head occasionally and smiled.

Once the school year started for Ophelia, we played in the afternoons and on weekends. Ophelia seemed to forget all her other friends. It wasn't long before Polonius started to worry that the playdate had been too successful. Polonius explained to her how, at our ages, we ought to be more interested in our own genders. With shrugging resignation she obeyed her parent and we saw less of each other. Going into default mode, I started inviting Rosencrantz and Guildenstern over again. During the summer, those two had grown and had grown even more indistinguishable. I was the ever-smaller third wheel, again convenient target of their jokes. But gradually I got used to it all, and my friendship with that slim smart girl seemed but a dream. When Ophelia and I did see each other, at a Christmas party or a dinner, her soft smile told me nothing had changed, nor would it ever.

Months passed I didn't see Ophelia at all. She started competing in dressage and made a new set of giggling, monomaniacal ponytailed friends. When she turned twelve, she was advanced a grade and sent to a proper all-girls boarding school in Massachusetts, where they probably throw tied sheets out the windows for the townie boys at night. That was that.

September 2009. I have not seen Ophelia in three years. In my memory she remains exactly as she was the last time I saw her, standing in the doorway of her father's home wearing her favorite dress, deep plum with pearls on the hem and short sleeves (it was very cold), waving as Gertrude and I pulled away. All this time she has been a main character in that old drama, My Lost Childhood, which I remember when the weather changes, smell violets, or go to a natural history museum.

Then suddenly last spring, while I was unpacking my things at that beastly Wittenberg dorm, living with a bunch of rude spoiled children (all older than I), I thought of her, powerfully. The recollection of those afternoons on Silo Ridge, with the wind in the white pines, came crashing back with a flood of endorphins. Was it because I found myself so alone for the first time? I sat down on my miserable bed and wondered in a panic if I had a saved image of her somewhere. Yes, yes, I did, the two of us at the county fair after the auction, standing next to that pathetic cow. (What became of that beast? I hardly remember.) The photo does not record the perfection of her complexion, the thinness of her skin, and she is making a droll face. But there she is, my Ophelia, still wearing her riding britches that she had donned in the early hours of that day, after lying awake thinking (of me?). And I am standing by her, shoulders touching, holding her hand. (I'm wearing a second-hand Sex Pistols T-shirt—from cousin Bryant—and skinny jeans. Oh, Gertrude, with your stage-set perfect aesthetics, why did you let me dress myself the day of my one and only photo of her?)

Suddenly I could not imagine a future without Ophelia. We would live together in my home as soon as she was old enough to marry. She would be fifteen now. In three years, Gertrude must give up the master bedroom for the new lord and lady. My mind raced, and I felt deliciously nervous, just as I did every time we had lain down on the mountain grass.

Maybe I could endure the next three years with the social media scholars after all, since I had to kill time waiting for Ophelia. Everyone at university was there for networking mainly, hoping to get into finance. No one could give a codpiece for Shakespeare. It was all getting me very depressed. I was studying history, to continue family tradition. Although I did not see Hamlet standing in front of students, boring them with his dry, insanely detailed lectures (particularly thorough on dates), I did imagine myself writing a four-volume series on some special remote corner of the past, visiting sites like my father did, decrypting old letters in little libraries in quaint towns, relating my intellectual adventures to my wife at dinner. Pass the beets and kale, my dear Ophelia. How lovely you look in salmon.

I sent a real paper love letter addressed to Ophelia at boarding school, a crazy letter, full of ridiculous idealism maybe, but I had license to write it.

> Doubt thou the stars are fire;
> Doubt that the sun doth move;
> Doubt truth to be a liar;
> But never doubt I love.
> Oh dear Ophelia, I am ill at these numbers;
> I have not art to reckon my groans: but that
> I love thee best, Oh most best, believe it. Adieu.
> Thine evermore most dear lady,
> whilst this machine is to him.
>   -Hamlet

She never replied. Her silence roared like the white pines in my dreams as I lay in my narrow bed in my narrow cell in Ohio. I was soon heartbroken and embarrassed over sending the letter, feeling misplaced, untethered. Then I came home for summer break and found Claudius's size eight shoes under my mother's bed, his slope-shouldered coats in the closet. Misfortune comes in threes, they say. Now, after the wedding, it dawns on me that my home, that rollicking cottage on the hill, might not be mine. I realized what I want in life precisely at the moment it became clear it was an unrealistic dream.

Now I lock my tree house door and half squat in a low camp chair, twirling a twig. The old tree limbs spearing the roof creak in the wind, and there in the eaves is that old stuffed egret, one leg missing and some of the feathers gone, but it still stares down at me with its black pearl eyes. There is hardly any point in returning to Wittenberg, now that I'm not the landed gent I thought I was. No economic future in a history degree. I can't have a wife like Ophelia on an independent scholar's income. Must go into business and start riding the train to the city.

I thought I had love, a house, with property. Wasn't the insurance settlement for me? Was I not the man of the house?

Now suddenly, holy shit, I may have to move out. I may have to get going on a real career (downloading templates for a CV) and apply online for a mortgage to buy my own split-level ranch, with wall-to-wall.

I wrap myself up in my swinging cocoon and wonder, should I pupate out of this life? Everything is not what I assumed it might be. But what if we are no caterpillars and our coffins no cocoons? What then? Awesome nothingness, one supposes. More terrible to me, at least for now, than my vague future, with its bland outlines and dull hazy details.

Where is Ophelia? Why won't she write me? Who is this man in my house with my mother? And why have I been out of my mind for eight years?

Act II

Chapter Six
Murder!

September 12, 2009. While my mother and her new paramour are away besmirching the sheets of that fine inn in Rhinebeck, I am back in the house, tending to chores. It is good to be "home" again while they are away, but my relocated bed on the upper floor is like a dry docked boat for my dreamless nights.

Today's chore is not pleasant. Pluto, the old long-horned ram, is to be slaughtered. He is the lead ram, with devilishly lined pupils, defiant and watchful; the others depend on his cynicism for survival. His ears are first to flick at the jangle of dog tags. He runs; they follow. He is long-legged and slender—when shorn—and like a noble king in his ample winter furs. But today he is to die.

Thing is, I am a carnivore, like most of our dominant species. I could toss plastic-wrapped flesh into my cart without thinking of the animal that spent its life standing in feces, shot full of antibiotics, miserable, unloved, alone. Or I can keep a small flock in verdant pastures, kill three a year when they get a little past middle age, after eight or nine years.

We never kill the lambs, thank god. Our breed are good meat sheep at a mature age. And I never do the slaughtering myself, though I take responsibility. I send for the mobile butcher unit, three Guatemalans with long curved knives. They have a supernatural way of calming the animals. They will slit his throat swiftly and murmur softly to him as he faints and dies. As pay they only want the *cojones* to grill and the head for soup.

The day is bright and cool, and the men with the cold shiny knives get out of their van with them already drawn, sharpening them as they approach the victim. If I were making a cartoon of a slaughter it might go this way.

Life comes with many unhappy compromises as packing material to keep the fragile stuff from breaking. On slaughter days, I am tempted to renounce carnivorous ways, and sometimes I can't eat the meat for a week, until the miasma of murder clears. Everyone should suffer so much every time he eats a burger. There would be less meat eaten. But, I must admit, after only a few weeks, the smell of roast mutton makes my mouth water again.

I've already separated Pluto from the others. I put him in a fresh pasture where he is excited about the long tender grass and does not care yet that the rest of his flock is on the other side of the fence. I leave the men to do their work, walking up the steps to the cottage without looking back.

Inside I read. Although I don't mean to, I find my eyes turning to look out the window, which frames the slaughter like a TV screen. Pluto is down, and the three men crouch around him. His legs are not kicking; they hold his flanks. He lifts his head from the ground a bit, and one of the men leans his face down to whisper in his ear; another strokes his fleece. Pluto lays his head down again quietly.

Poor Pluto. I remember when he was a lamb, a coiled spring of life. From a standing position, he could jump three feet in the air. His horns started growing while he was still in the womb, and he was a difficult birth for his mother. He started butting me when he was just a week old.

Down the driveway now I see a black SUV pull up and stop. Polonius gets out, then so does Laertes, whom I have not seen in three or four years. He is wearing desert fatigues and aviator sunglasses, as if he has stepped out of Ophelia's photographs. With broad shoulders and a jaw like a pit bull, he is superhuman, especially next to his frail father. As they walk up the steps, I watch them to see if they have caught sight of the slaughter in the field. No, they don't notice.

I am standing at the sink washing my hands when I hear Polonius knock three times loudly before letting himself in. I meet them in the dim, cramped foyer and flick on the light.

"Oh, you're home Hamlet."

"Yes, while he's gone I'm lord of the manor again."

"Your mother asked me to come over to pick up some papers. Oh, here they are." He picks up an envelope, on which my mother has written "Polonius" in big florid script, mimicking his own hand. Parody or flattery, I cannot tell. Gertrude does seem fond of the geezer.

Polonius is having trouble finding his breast pocket. "You remember Laertes," he says as he finally slips the envelope in. With patient smiles, Laertes and I have both been watching him struggle with his task.

"I do. He is even larger in life than I remember him to be."

Laertes responds with some perfectly appropriate greeting, all respect and courtesy. This is just as I expected.

"You've been in a long time. Are you done now or just on leave?"

"Five years," he says, glancing at his father. "It's done."

"Good," I say nodding. "That's good," and I pat him on the back.

"He has literally just flown in. I picked him up at the airport about an hour ago," says Polonius. "Unfortunately, since his arrival was a bit of a surprise, I have to take care of some business before we get back home. I'm dragging him around with me." He nudges Laertes. "Well, I've got to get the notary before she goes home. Ready Laertes. Good seeing you Hamlet."

Neither turn to go. Laertes has taken off his sunglasses. His sunburnt face is marked by pale crow's feet that fan out of the corners of his eyes, like war paint across his high cheekbones. It is hard to imagine just how intensely one would have to squint to form wrinkles deep enough to block the sun so completely. They both stand there staring at me, Polonius with his usual eaglelike focus and Laertes as if he is looking through me at the wall. I feel nudged by invisible stage directions. "Why don't you stay with me while Polonius does his errands. Trust me with him Polonius?"

Polonius opens his mouth but nothing comes out.

Leading them both through the center hall into the kitchen I ask, "Do you want something to drink? I'm afraid we don't have beer—no wait, Claudius must have some," peering into the fridge. "Yes, how about a Two Xes?"

"You shouldn't drink," says Polonius tiredly.

"I am feeling jet-lagged. It will only make it worse."

"I don't drink the stuff either. How about a cappuccino then?"

Polonius sees that I've taken over the situation, and he turns toward the foyer.

"Good-bye Dad."

"Polonius," I say, waving.

"Back soon," he sings and is out the door.

I get two cups down from the cupboard and start hand-grinding coffee beans. "What's up with him?"

"Most of us get a good prescription when we're ready to ship home." Laertes, offering his help, grips the grinder with machinelike claws and cranks the handle effortlessly. His suggestion of vulnerability does not align with his demonstrable brute strength.

"You seem to be the same Laertes I remember. There was nothing you couldn't do well." Against my will I wonder how I might rate in Ophelia's mind against such a measure of manliness.

Laertes has turned and is looking around the kitchen for a prop to handle so that he can appear natural and nonchalant. He strokes an old hand pump we have for our farmhouse sink. "This work?"

His nervousness has thrown me. I have the urge to treat him kindly, a big lion with a thorn in his paw. "It does." I demonstrate by working the lever up and down, eventually a cold stream comes coughing up. "This is more convenient most of the time," I say turning on and off the regular faucet, "but it's good to have a pump when the electricity goes out. It does often around here—the trees you know. Can't understand why they don't bury power lines. Habit I suppose."

"You have a great old house, lots of character."

"You know your father found it for us. He keeps at it too, helping. He strives for indispensability. So what about the medication?" I ask ,getting back to his remark, which, it seemed, he didn't just throw out there for me to ignore.

"Oh, standard issue, part of reentry procedure." Laertes shrugs.

"Look, I know that father of yours pretty well. His bumbling awkwardness is just a smokescreen. I can tell when he's up to something. He brought you here to drop you off. Out with it, brother."

My calling him "brother" is the thorn removed. He softens and looks at me directly almost with a kind of love. "Hamlet is all grown up now, I see."

"Does it show that much? I tried to stay in a state of blissful denial. But it didn't work."

"I was saying things to Polonius on the drive he didn't want to hear. He needed to get rid of me for a while so that he could marshal his counterarguments."

"Ah yes. For an eavesdropper, he is not much of a listener."

"A busybody."

"Oh well," I reply, glad not to have been the one to say it. We take our cups through the center hall and into the dining room, a many tall-windowed room, more like a wide corridor, that connects the oldest part of the house to one of its several additions. He sits at the head of the long narrow table (because that's the kind of man he is), and I sit to his left with the corner between us. "I haven't seen Ophelia in years, but we were close as kids. You don't grow out of that."

"No."

"Is she well?" I ask with high-pitched fake indifference.

"I think she is. I haven't seen her yet. She's up at boarding school."

"Yes, I knew that. And will she be coming back soon to see her brother?" I ask, hoping.   Her smiling brother does not miss it.

I see a resemblance to Ophelia haunting the wide shape of his eyes, and I find it somewhat disconcerting. "I'm sure she is on her way."

"She still like horses?"

"No, she grew out of that."

"Really?" I never much appreciated her horse hobby, but it pains me to hear that she has changed in any way. "Do you take sugar?"

"No, thank you. She is still just a kid, you know."

Staring ahead, I say in monotone, "Under eighteen. I am painfully aware that I have lately crossed the border into adulthood without her."

"Just being the older brother."

"Understood." We pause while I remember my old jealousy. Perhaps it goes both ways.   "Sometimes I feel responsible," I say, returning to the war topic, "for everyone who gets hurt over there, for me." The "for me" squeezed out like a wincing stepchild.

Laertes smiles lightly.

My eyes tear up. "Here I am eight years later crying about it."

"You know what the VA says about the suicides? They blame it on money troubles and cheating spouses. I have neither. Do you know what you were patting me on the back for just now?"

"Thanking you for what you did over there."

"What we did? We beheaded Saddam's statue and then roasted weenies on the riot fires until Baghdad was nothing but smoldering piles of mud brick. Centuries of progress utterly wiped out—no clean water, no electricity, no food supplies, no hospitals, not even a mattress free of debris for a family to sleep on." His tone is ironic, careless, like a guest on a talk show promoting his new situation comedy. "Did you know that the second heart transplant in history was performed in Baghdad? That's all gone. In one generation, education completely obliterated." Laertes scratches his cropped head with his iron claw, then uses it to daintily pick up his cappuccino cup. "I'll tell you, it was like nobody had planned a damn thing. That's not the US military." This he adds with wounded pride. "We don't go into places unless we know exactly what we want to do."

"Your father didn't want to hear that, I take it?"

"It is unfortunately true. Then one day a couple of months ago I woke up to the sound of shelling and, just like that, I realized that was the plan. We are not there to build roads to freedom, educate the girls. We are there to cause chaos, to strike at the foundations of the whole damned ancient culture."

"I am ignorant of most things that lie beyond the bounds of my nutshell." I'd always assumed it was more rewarding being in the hero business than the fool business, but today I do not envy Laertes. I wish I could come up with a good line, but I can find nothing appropriate to say to this mass of muscle and teeth whose heart is clearly breaking.

I listen to Laertes continue to tell me about his tours. It is a long, terrible confession, and about the worst things he did, he only hints. Sitting back in his chair, he looks out the window. Years of compressed guilt-frustration come out at once, and I wonder if I am his first. Would he have been able to talk to fellow soldiers or is that sort of thing against code?

As a boy it seemed to me that the victims' families were less keen than the general public to crack some Arab heads after 9/11, but they didn't really ask for our opinion. I confess to Laertes that I stopped paying attention to the news when I realized the government is not troubled by the bleating of its flock. "Personally, I would have preferred a civilized investigation, the UN directing the hunt for bin Laden, and an international court deciding his fate after weighing the evidence, not the never-ending Dodge City shoot-out we got."

"I don't know what the brass does to get themselves to sleep," he sighs. "They're either sociopaths or they have some twisted greater good theory, which amounts to the same thing, I guess. Say anything. That is how they do it. As long as some authority figure dismisses the accusations, that's the end of the conversation. No one checks the facts or wants to hear about it. My own father is happy to have me just take my medication."

I try to be encouraging. "I feel like it's the end of an era, a new president, troops returning, the dead forgotten, a new husbandfather."

"Only it isn't ending. You can't kill terrorism. It is like a hydra: cut off one head and seven more will take its place. Now the eye is turning homeward."

We hear Polonius coming in the door. "Guess who is here," he calls.

As Laertes and I get up and go to the kitchen, a simulacrum of Ophelia advances into view. Her hair is dyed red. Her eyes are ringed like a raccoon's in purple shadow, and she is wearing a black scratchy synthetic dress that is too tight across her ribcage and too low on her hips. She is a big girl now, easily half again my weight. Her face and her body, though recognizable, are so changed. I look, wondering, with my jaw chattering. And then she begins to smile nervously; I remember in an instant everything I ever loved about her. Oh, my dear beautiful Ophelia!

80

"Laertes!" she turns to her brother first. I step aside and let the pair embrace while I hold my elbows, the image of jealousy.

Now it's my turn. Her body is warm and her cheek cool. The same Ophelia smell, masked a little by deodorant and hair goo, sends me to heaven.

"Hamlet," she says with less enthusiasm. "There are three devils outside hanging a carcass in that big tree."

"Poor Pluto," I say.

"The little lamb?" replies Ophelia as if the intervening years had never happened. Her voice is familiar and more and more of that slim smart girl rematerializes before me.

"He was an agèd ram. You do eat meat, I remember, and you were never squeamish about carcasses. Do you want the fleece? It will be a soft plush one, black and curly."

"Sure," she shrugs. "Though I don't do that anymore. I mean, hang on to things."

I widen my eyes at her.

"Are you slaughtering lambs? I must have missed that on my way in," says Laertes.

Not surprising, think I.

"Ophelia," says Laertes, "you promised to write me every day. I only heard from you once a week."

"That's not true. I wrote every day."

"Posting to your Facebook wall is not writing to me. Your lines are charming, sometimes too charming, and obviously not directed at me. Is Hamlet a 'friend'?"

"He is."

"Then be a good girl and take him off," says Laertes. Ophelia throws her eyes up to the ceiling and folds her arms. "Only family men and boys under eighteen."

"Oh," says Ophelia. "Do men sometimes have dark thoughts?"

What a crazed family. Polonius now is leering at me. Laertes's hand is moving to his hilt. "There is no darkness where Ophelia is. Besides I don't think you ever 'friended' me," I say.

"No?" she seems genuinely surprised.

"I wrote by stamped mail. Maybe you don't remember," I say.

"Oh yes. I meant to send you a friend invite."

My heart is punctured and bleeding. "It doesn't matter. You would be entirely underwhelmed by my Facebook activity," I say.

Polonius nods approvingly. "Too much time online is a distracting experience," *(theatrical pause)*. Actually, I'm glad you bring it up, as I have found that I have something to say Laertes. I might as well say it now. Hamlet is family."

"I appreciate that, but if this something Laertes might —"

Polonius ignores me and goes right on talking, "I looked at several of your Facebook items, and learned of your continued debasement of the Iraqi war effort. Also, I looked at videos you posted about it all being part of an oil industry conspiracy, from which I ranged to more Internet-based polemics, the usual claim-counterclaim kind of stuff." Polonius looks over the heads of his children. "None of this resonates with me, so I keep a respectful distance. I do not wish to join the conspiracy conversation."

"You don't have to 'like' my posts, Father."

"There are other positions you have taken, on Ron Paul for example, which I do not take. It is not part of the person I am to require those I care about to be aligned with me on things I believe. I hope I engender reciprocal courtesy, which allows me to think freely in directions I choose."

"I didn't think you were part of the conversation," says Laertes.

"You left your computer in the car."

Without changing his expression or saying anything, Laertes walks out. After a while we hear him open the car door. Keeping one eye on the window, Polonius leans into me speaking low. "Hamlet, I need you to do me a favor. Make friends with Laertes. He's been having trouble. Keep an eye on him. I don't like the things he's saying. I fear he could be suffering from post-traumatic stress disorder. PTSD. I don't want a son of mine to lose it, you know. Become part of some silly rebellion. So this is what you need to do."

Ophelia is looking at me, wincing, clearly feeling sorry for me.

"It's for his own good," Polonius goes on. "Join this Tea Party movement he's part of."

I have no idea what he's talking about. "Yes, absolutely."

"Feel him out. See what direction this group is going, whether it's gun rights, or building bunkers. If Laertes doesn't seem interested, then test him out. Say, hypothetically of course, 'Wouldn't it be nice if we could storm the capital or take over a TV station?' See how he responds to the idea. If he says, 'No we should never say such things against our government,' then all is well. If he listens, then draw him out further, if you get my mind."

"I'm one step ahead of you, Sir. I figured it out when you arranged this meeting here what you were up to." I glance at Ophelia. She is suppressing a smile. I smile back.

"Did you? That's clever."

"I'm a clever sort. Now here's what I've found. He's awfully stressed and all. But he's a good lad. Talked nonstop about girls, actually."

"Oh, that's good. That's a positive sign."

"He's as red and white as he is blue."

Laertes returns with a camouflage computer case under his arm and goes into the dining room, where he sits down. He says nothing. His face is expressionless.

"And hey," I go on brightly, "if the oil companies happen to do well as an indirect result of all of our freedom fighting, who could complain?" I put my arm around Polonius. "And so millions will be made by a few, and they'll make more, those alchemists. Meanwhile we are belly up to the trough, no?"

Polonius nods in agreement, but isn't quite sure.

"Are we not all better off now, in general? Don't we all have more than we really need, soft around the middle," I pat Polonius's belly, and he waves me away, disgusted. "A little dull in spirit, distracted. But entertained, vaccinated, shorn, dehorned, dewormed, domesticated animals have got it better than the wild sort. The free face deprivation, starve in winter. Their coats are shaggy and lifespans short. They're full of ticks and burrs, stinking like themselves. Fresh straw in the barn looks relatively inviting, huh?"

Polonius is still assenting, but he looks a bit peeved.

"None of it is possible, has ever been possible, without war. Wealth gets created. Sometimes soldiers have to shoot mothers and children, lambs have to be sacrificed, fathers' skulls crushed—to knit the community together. A little killing can't hurt, in the overall picture, right Laertes?"

"I think that's how it goes," he says without turning.

"Right." I say with confidence. "See, your son is fine," I whisper in Polonius's ear.

Polonius wobbles his head side to side to show he's not so sure. Laertes doesn't move. Ophelia is waiting.

"I have an idea," I say, clapping my hands together. "We've got to keep Laertes awake until bedtime, right? I haven't seen Ophelia in three years, and she owes me some time because she promised once to be mine forever, we all need a little cheering up, and Polonius has things to do, so why don't I take your children, Polonius, up to Poland for a little fun. I was planning to go anyway. It's market day. Tomorrow it comes to Amenia, but it's better there."

"Gertrude does the market," explains Polonius, irrelevantly.

"Yes, fleece and wool batten, eggs sometimes. But she and Claudius are still in Rhinebeck."

"For their honeymoon?" asks Ophelia.

"Right," I say, showing my displeasure. "But it is bad form to say such things about someone's mother."

"Hamlet don't—" chides Ophelia, leveling her pretty green eyes at me.

"What? I am not the first son to resent remarriage. There is a great tradition. I am only feeling what convention compels me to."

Ophelia grins. It is not an innocent smile. She always was good at eye contact, only now that she's past puberty it does not have the same effect, of reassuring me of her honesty, that it used to have.

"You've both been gone awhile, and what did you citiots ever know anyway?" I continue. "A lot has changed in three years. It's really quite the scandal. They have their own currency in Poland, a kind of barter system. People worry it will spread like swine flu. Some hippies from Vermont started a vegetable co-op there, but they didn't count on the townspeople all being unemployed. Not wanting their produce to rot, they sold it for IOUs. When they needed carpentry or plumbing they traded them in. Ten years later . . . I know all this from the beeswax and honey lady who has the stall next to Gertrude's."

"I'm sure there are laws against it. They'll crack down on it eventually. Not a lot of taxes are collected there," says Polonius.

"Oh, what do I know about economics? I'm a simple shepherd." Ophelia and Laertes look at each other and then their father. "Shall we? I'll drive."

Polonius opens his mouth, but nothing comes out. Laertes rises and picks up his computer bag. "Sounds like it could be fun. Coming Ophelia?"

"Of course," she says, eye contact again, smile.

"Sorry old man, the young'uns need their time alone. You'll be all right won't you?" I whisper, "Like we planned," and raise my brows at him. "Hm?"

On the car ride north, Ophelia sits shotgun. Her bulky brother gallantly offered to fold himself up in the back of my Mercedes (I drive the old diesel sedan that was my father's, 350,000 miles and still puttering along). I take the old windy road, each bend of which shows a different postcard view. Purple ironweed grows in bunches in the ditches alongside the road intermixed with sprays of various yellow wildflowers, cut-stone walls, crumbling in places, run up and down the hills, large estates sprawl with giant horses or shaggy-haired Scottish cattle ornamenting the lawns, and little dilapidated trailers with smoke rising from crooked stovepipes occupy the lots on the corners near the road.

Laertes is angry. "He pisses me off. He says, *I don't require those I care about to be aligned with me. I hope I engender reciprocal courtesy, and you will allow me to think freely in directions I choose.* Is he threatened because I have an opinion?"

"There does seem to be a note of offense in his defense," I say.

"He's just getting old, especially in the last few years. He repeats himself constantly," says Ophelia.

"Old men are like crabs, they go backward and become great babies again," I say.

"I am the one who is not being allowed to think freely. Isn't saying something part of thinking? Or am I supposed to just keep it to myself?"

"Say it, but say it slant. That's my approach," I say.

"If I don't tell it like it is, it just goes on."

"It'll go on anyway," says Ophelia to her brother.

"He doesn't even know what I think. He doesn't listen. What did I ever say about Ron Paul, other than he doesn't want unnecessary war?"

"I suggest that we be good Americans and drop all the serious discussions. Laertes is interested in politics. He knows more than I do and has an opinion. I haven't really left home yet and am in no hurry to do so." I look for Laertes's reaction in the rearview mirror. He folds his arms and stares out the window.

"My father said you were living in your tree house," says Ophelia.

"I am, when the new man of the house is there. When the weather gets really cold I'll decide what to do next. Maybe they will get an apartment in the city. That is a hope anyway. We'll see who's more patient. I could take a wife and people the house with lots of children, drive them away. Huh, Ophelia?" I glance again at unhappy Laertes. "We have plenty of time for you to bring me up to speed on world politics."

Addressing my reflection in the mirror Laertes asks, "Did you listen to what I said earlier about Ophelia?"

"What about Ophelia," asks Ophelia.

"Your brother reminded me that I'm eighteen and you're fifteen."

"That's *so* ridiculous, Laertes," whines Ophelia childishly.

In Poland the farmers' market is thick with slow-moving crowds, a mix of L.L. Bean catalog and Woodstock off-the-rack. It is a fine September day, sky clear, air clean and crisp, after a good wet, warm growing season. The harvest abounds. We glance at the stalls. Laertes buys honey for Ophelia with a hundred dollar bill and gets change in local currency.

"Souvenir," he says and puts the change in his pocket. "My friend Ron would approve. Have you been home yet Ophelia? Should we get some groceries?"

She says her father probably expects her to do the shopping. As brother and sister discuss menus, choose vegetables and cheeses, I notice a dark shape advancing. "That guy is not from around here," I say, pointing out Carlyle Hogg bulldozing his way through the crowd. "It's the lunch lady's husband. He's some kind of Blackwater man now, I hear."

As Hogg approaches them, Ophelia and I step off the curb to let him pass.

"Why, if it isn't Mr. Hogg."

"Who are you?" he asks rudely, snarling.

"Hamlet. You must remember my mother, Gertrude."

Hogg laughs in a menacing way that reminds me of corrupt cops in gangster movies, a deep chuckle that devolves into a desperate wheeze, eyes watering. He seems genuinely, if sinisterly, amused to see me, as if he thinks my making my way into adulthood is funny.

"These are my friends, Ophelia and Laertes."

Hogg's gaze passes right over Ophelia, but he looks at Laertes approvingly. "Just get home son?"

"In fact yes, just," replies Laertes, who has not moved out of Hogg's way.

"Welcome home. I gave twelve years to my country. Desert Shield."

Laertes does not reply. He has not been asked a question.

"You in Iraq?"

"Yes, Sir," he says, perfectly correctly, but I can feel the sarcasm. He probably suspects that he outranks Hogg, though he's half his age.

"Damn shame they're bringing the men back now. The minute we're out of there the radical groups will come back in, and then it will be even worse."

Laertes appears not to have been listening, which I am relieved to see. He hasn't taken off his sunglasses, but I think he is staring over Hogg's shoulder. Finally he says, "It was nice meeting you Mr. Hoag."

"That's Hogg," Hogg corrects.

"Of course," says Laertes, with such dry delivery I am envious.

After Hogg goes on, Laertes asks, "Who is that man? I don't trust him."

"No? Can't imagine why not. He is treated like a minor god in Amenia, but he probably gets bullied himself by the really big guys." I glance back to see Hogg's blocky shape parting the sea of people. "I don't believe he is wanting organic greens. Here to cause some sort of mischief no doubt."

"You can't make fun of him because he's fat," says my chubby Ophelia.

"It is not his literal fatness that I mind, my dear. But thanks for being concerned about my moral center. It is the figurative way he throws his weight around and puts the squash on well-meaning little folk such as my mother."

We continue through the market toward the coffee shop in the back of the library. The oldest building in town, the brick structure spills over into adjoining buildings so one has to work one's way through a maze of book stacks to get to the café. I have noted on several occasions that the "new book" section features more local writers than national ones, which seems just the right touch. The library is done up in time-capsule theme, decorated with stuffed wildlife that speaks of a diversity that no longer exists in these parts: stranger great grey owls, jewel-like hook bills, enormous jackrabbits, panthers. The specimen cases are a gift of Mr. Pease, the moose and mouse gifts of Mrs. Josiah Cadwallader and so on. The backs of several of the chairs read, "In loving memory of Cecilia Rakestraw" and other old-fashioned names, like so many tombstones, reaffirming the theme, of all libraries, of death and living memory. The spines on the biography shelves, I realize, are also like tombstones.

"This is cool," says Ophelia.

"Of course you think it's cool."

Ophelia frowns. "I was a pretty weird kid."

"I love you that way," I whisper, taking her hand for a moment.

"I don't have any of my specimens anymore. I buried them all a few years ago."

"Buried them, really? That seems unnecessary."

She shrugs. "I wanted to move on, but now I'm a little sorry."

"There's no real solution; move on, hang on, one is not better than the other. Hey," I say, changing the subject, "I think that you, Miss Young Person—since, as your brother reminds us, you are underage—I think you will like the little music scene here, and there may even be some music tonight, if you want to stay late."

"I can't. Not tonight."

"Another time then. I will keep after you."

She smiles and tosses her eyebrow up in a way that seems to suggest I might be allowed to keep trying. Little does Laertes know that my virginity is probably the only one at risk between us two, since hers, methinks, is long gone. Something about the way she looks at me says so.

Nodding my head at the café music, I say, "It's a local band they're playing now. They're great. They have beards and dress in drag. Musical diversity, that's the thing."

Laertes has gone off to the counter. I can tell he likes being the older brother, to Ophelia, and maybe to me too.

"My mom and I just missed this. We bought a little too far to the south. Their public school is a progressive one-room schoolhouse, where the older kids tutor the younger ones. They sit on beanbag chairs. They play sports but don't keep score. The community center takes care of teen moms, helps illegals with paperwork, weeds senior citizens' gardens and repairs their houses. They shuttle the poor to doctor appointments.

"The businesses here are all employee-owned, so the corporate body does indeed include the feet, the gut, the head, the bent back. The nonprofit hospital, which has always been good and has since gotten much better, sells modest sliding-scale memberships, which cover wellness checks and catastrophic illness. The town recycles almost all the waste, including human manure, from which methane is extracted to provide gas for everyone's heat in winter. Nothing sold here has been through a large factory. All the glass jars, like the milk bottles, are returned to the farmers' market and reused. The local artists, musicians and writers actually make a living here. Chickens and guinea hens roam free, eating ticks, eliminating the Lyme disease that is an epidemic everywhere else in Dutchess County. The restaurants feature only local produce. The bars serve local microbrew."

"Hamlet, I think you're making it all up," says Ophelia dryly.

"Just the part about the beer. They do make their own wine though."

Laertes brings back a tray with three slices of pumpkin pie, two hot ciders and a black coffee for himself. "I like this little town," he says.

"Look, a guinea hen." I point to the courtyard through the window. "See, you thought I was making it up. I was just telling Ophelia they have a lot of things right here. Amenia is lagging behind a bit, but we've gotten better, especially in the last few years. There are still folks like Mr. Hogg who resent it all. He must *hate* Poland. I wonder why he was here."

On the way out, we discover why. Hogg is back with two deputies from the sheriff's department brutally busting a baker for not collecting sales tax and confiscating all his goods.

On the drive to return the siblings home, all the ingested caffeine in the world cannot keep Laertes from falling asleep in the backseat, which I'm certain he would never do in a foxhole (do they still have such things in war?), but here he finally feels safe.

We take the new road back south, straight, with only two or so traffic lights. Ophelia and I are hypnotized by the yellow line, tired, not very talkative.

"Do you ever wonder," asks Ophelia after a while, "if some day you might just jerk the wheel a little bit and go straight into oncoming traffic?"

"What? And kill myself?" I ask.

"I don't mean really. It's just weird to think that it would be so easy to do it. You don't ever worry sometimes that you might just twitch?"

"No," I reply gently. "Never. And you?"

She smiles. "No," she says, in a way that sounds like "no, silly."

"It's a terrible thought. Don't think it anymore. Okay Ophelia?"

"Okay," she says, very childishly. I want to hold her very badly. Poor Ophelia, my poor mad Ophelia.

When we pull into their dark driveway, we find the gate closed. I roll down my window to get to the keypad. "What is the code?" I whisper.

She whispers back, "Four, six, two, eight."

"Now I can sneak in any time I want and knock on your window. Four, six, two, eight," I say, as I enter the code. "That spells 'goat'."

Ophelia frowns and shrugs. "It's Dad's code. I never asked what it spelled. It's just like you to think about it."

"Just like me, huh?"

The gates swing open, and we go down the long driveway and park below the house, a grand affair with stone columns and a pretentious statue of a nymph in the garden. Polonius has left the porch light on. We sit for a long time wondering if Laertes will wake, my leather jacket squeaking softly on the leather seats, as I reach to put my arm around her.

"Love will burn the furniture to keep warm," she whispers cryptically. I'm not sure if I should agree, so I just brush her hair back from her face and look at her. She is very pretty in the dim dashboard light. She leans toward me, across Laertes's line of view, were he awake, and kisses me once very softly. On cue, Laertes rouses himself.

"Good morning," says Ophelia.

"I fell asleep," Laertes explains in an almost drunken accent.

They get out of the car promising to do it again soon and walk arm in arm up the bluestone steps to their mausoleum-like home.

Chapter Seven
Hark
Seek for thy noble father in the dust
—*Hamlet*, Act I, scene ii

September 13, 2009. It is Sunday afternoon, and I am at the Amenia Farmers' Market managing Gertrude's stall while she is still away on her misadventure with Claudius. It is a windy day, and not many customers have come. I am staring into the far distance, into the field beyond the parking lot, waiting for someone to rouse me about some wool, when a welcomed face materializes out of the blur, a clean-shaven handsome face, a man in his late forties, just going grey, with masculine jaw, fashionable glasses like Brooklyn academics wear, carrying two heavy book bags. "It's Mr. Horatio or I am hallucinating. I don't blame you if you don't recognize me. I've had eight growth spurts since."

"I would recognize you anywhere, Hamlet," he replies. "Even covered in white dust."

"That's true. That's the last I saw you. How have you been?" He offers his hand, but I grab his arm with both hands, pull him toward me and embrace him heartily. We step back and look at each other smiling, as the wind plays with our hair.

"Maybe you can see young Hamlet lurking here still. Same shock of black hair in my eyes, same gap-toothed smile, skinny legs."

He looks me up and down approvingly. Then he glances around at my table, with baskets of tricolored wool batten and soft white fleeces.

"But even more to the point," I go on, "why are you here in Amenia? We'll teach you to eat toaster waffles for dinner before you go home."

"I'm here for vacation, and I heard about the market."

"Don't mock me. You're passing through. It is a beautiful place to see from your car. But it is all for show, like the fake Soviet villages, to make you think the rural life here is sane when it's not. Amenia has terrible secrets."

Horatio laughs briefly, then he puts his hand on my shoulder. "Hamlet. I'm sorry about your father. I never got to say so."

"Yeah, Mom whisked us off as soon as the airlines were running again."

"I understand. You must miss your father. I know you were close."

"Were we? It's hard for me to tell. I was just a kid."

"It seemed so to me. He was one of the few fathers who came in for parent-teacher meetings."

My eyes water and I squeeze them hard. I press the heels of my palms into my eyes and take a deep breath. "I do miss him. Horatio, I think I hear my father, sometimes, while

I'm lying in bed on Saturday mornings. I think I hear him making breakfast like he used to do."

Horatio puts an arm around me, just like he did that day he found me by the bridge.

"Should we go get coffee after you're done here? I think the market is closing soon?"

"Sure. It'll only take me a few minutes to pack up my table and tent."

Horatio offers to help. My car is parked behind the table with the trunk open. We load the baskets and disassemble the tent poles.

"You raise sheep?"

"Yeah, pretty hilarious, huh?"

"Well, a lot of people are doing it now, leaving the city, setting up little hobby farms."

"I don't know how Gertrude and I have managed to become hip by being so completely out of it."

"Have you? Not up on current events?"

"Well, yes and no. I've traveled everywhere, but we don't watch the news or keep up on celebrities."

Horatio nods and thinks a bit. He imitates me as I roll up fleece and store the batten in repurposed feedbags.

"Thrift," I explain.

"Thrift is the new elegance. Does your mother spin?"

I laugh at the thought of Gertrude staying still that long. "No, we outsource it to shut-ins, people too sick—too big in most cases—to get out and around. Gives them an income."

"I noticed the obesity problem when I stopped at the gas station."

"Yeah, well they have access to veggies. They just don't come to the market. It's mostly the citiots."

"The what?"

"Citiots. It's what the locals call the weekenders who come up from the city."

"People like me, in other words?"

"Precisely."

"Ouch."

"Why don't we go to my farm? It's not far. There is only one café in town, and they close at two."

"Where do you get your three o'clock coffee?"

"Yes, I know. It's difficult in the sticks."

Horatio follows my car in his. When we arrive back at the farm, four ewes are trotting up the driveway about to go into the road. I roll down my window. "Ladies, where are you going?" They freeze, and their ears twitch around. Such poise. So alert.

"Should I get out to help?" calls Horatio from his car. He has pulled into the drive behind me.

"No, as much as I might like to see a citiot try. We can shepherd them with our cars."

The sheep run to the side of the road to let the cars pass, and then they file in behind and trot back to the house after us.

"That's incredible," says Horatio, slamming his car door, watching the sheep return to the pasture.

"They're sheep," I say laughing. "They follow."

"It must have been great growing up in the country."

"Maybe I've missed a lot. I wouldn't know."

Looking up at the cottage as we mount the worn stone steps, I suddenly became aware of its relative shabbiness; the shutter on an upper bedroom window sags on one hinge and the thyme ground cover is claiming the path.

"This is really lovely, Hamlet."

"We got it cheap from some bankrupt Keebler Elves. It's a bit ramshackle, but it's my home, or at least I've thought so. I never imagined Gertrude would remarry. But she has, *on the eleventh*." I wait, allowing Horatio to take in that piece of information. "He has a horrible laugh too, Horatio. Just a disaster socially. He is a bureaucratic engineer."

"I'm an engineer."

"You're a teacher. That's different."

"I *was* a science teacher. I went back to school. Now I'm an engineer."

"Oops," I say, noting that Horatio is the best-looking engineer I can ever remember meeting. He looks more like a poet (and less like an elementary school teacher than I remember).

"It's okay. I know what you mean. He has a pocket protector and gets his home furnishings at Staples."

"Ah, yes, well you overshoot the mark with the pocket protector, but yeah, he's just terrible, unimaginative, and I don't see why Gertrude would have lunch with him much less—" Awkward silence follows.

We go into the stone-tiled foyer that is old and pitted granite, the kind that used to line the sidewalks of town. Not original with the house, it is still ancient in American years. I sit down on an old worn painted bench to remove my boots and Horatio does the same beside me.

"And I can't stop dreaming about my father lately. Maybe his ghost is trying to get me to do something. I'm up all night with bad dreams. I even moved out to that tree house you saw there as we came in, and I'll probably camp out there again when they come back."

"It looks like a nice little fort, but it can't be that comfortable."

"I have a hammock, plenty of fresh air and night sounds."

We go into the living room, whose small north-facing windows, with deep casements, let in little light, about as much as keyholes in battlements do. I switch on two table lamps on either side of the sofa where I sit down. Horatio praises the coziness of the house again and seats himself in Gertrude's favorite dry leather chair that crackles with age.

"You know, you can talk to me about what happened to you after I dropped you off at home." He takes off his glasses and rubs his nose bridge. "Your mother is a fantastic woman, don't get me wrong, and she always loved you, maybe too much, but some people are better at some things than they are at others. Something tells me you didn't get a lot of emotional support . . . ?" He trails off there, and the last words are intoned with the uncertainty that he might be going in the wrong direction.

"Oh, I don't know. She probably did all right. That doesn't mean that I spent enough time with it." Horatio waits for me. I go on. "We don't know what he was doing there. He should have been uptown at his office. At first, we didn't imagine he *was* there, not until very late in the evening did we even begin to worry. There were waves of dusty survivors, trauma victims, witnesses coming over the bridge late into the night. We watched them from the window with binoculars. He would have had to walk a long way. So we waited. But he didn't come home that night. Mother checked the hospitals, though we were still pretty sure his cell was out and he was at a friend's. The next day he still wasn't home. We waited. I don't remember if it was the third or the fourth day that I made one of those fliers with his picture on it and stapled it to the wall near the train station. I don't know why

I did that. By that time there wasn't any hope left really, none at all."

"You never got a DNA confirmation?"

"No, nothing for us."

"Well there are a lot of people who were never identified, whose bodies disappeared, turned to dust. Seems hard to understand how it could have happened, but there weren't many bodies recovered, mostly just half-inch shards of dry bone."

"We didn't even get that. He's not dead for us, Horatio. He's just missing. He could come back at any moment, technically you know, since there is no evidence that he was there, no motive for him to have been there, as far as I know, no likelihood. But he was there, we have come to believe that. A strange application of faith, don't you think?"

Horatio smiles sadly.

"When do you take down a missing-person flier? It was still up months later. I passed by and saw it there and felt so pathetic, but I couldn't take it down. There were hundreds of fliers. They were fading, curling up at the edges, colors were running. The collage of them flapped in the wind like a tattered quilt. Every once in a while you would see one, blown loose, tumbling down the street. I heard on the news that a group of artists finally had the sense and decency to take them all down, carefully fold them up, and put them away. I was so grateful to them." Here I cannot resist the tears anymore. "Isn't it strange what makes you cry and what doesn't?" I sob. "I can talk about not having a body to bury just fine, but when I think about the kindness of some stranger, I go to pieces like a girl."

Horatio reaches across the living room table to snatch a tissue for me. "Hamlet, do you remember when I found you by the bridge?"

"I remember."

"We were all in shock that day."

"That day. That day. It's a tape on a loop in my head. It won't stop playing lately."

"You had scooped up some of the dust, and you were holding it in your hand, Hamlet. That's what I remember, how you held on to that dust as if it were something important."

I nod. Wiping the tears off my cheeks with the heels of my hands.

"You said you wanted to keep it, so I put it in that plastic bag I found. We found your cousin, and I walked you both across the bridge and took you home."

Again I nod. "I remember that you forgot to give it back to me."

"I did forget. I'm sorry, but I did keep it for you. I don't know why. It seemed important to you, and after I heard that your father had died, I couldn't throw it away. So I kept it somewhere safe. I always meant to give it back to you when I saw you again." He pulls a white plastic grocery bag out of his leather book satchel.

Could it really be that same bag? I feel strangely affected by it, as if it has some totemic power to transport me back eight years to that awful day. Horatio puts the bag on the table and looks at me very solemnly. I begin to wonder if I am not being led through some catechism.

"That dust turned out to be very important—Hamlet, you were right. I am not on vacation. I came up to find you."

Horatio's demeanor has changed. He stands up and goes to the window, while I sit crumpled on the sofa, damp wad of Kleenex in one hand. "You came up here to find me?"

He looks out the window and speaks with his back to me, like an actor in a film noir. "A few years ago I heard about a scientist who was looking for samples of the dust to run tests on. I gave it to him." He turns and sits down in the leather chair again. "Your sample, Hamlet, turned out to be crucial because you collected it right after." He pauses. "It tested for incendiaries."

"Incendiaries?" I say, confused.

"Yes, they found traces."

"Like explosives?"

"Yes."

"You're saying there were bombs in the buildings too."

"Something like that. It is pretty clear, the way they came down. That wasn't a collapse."

"Okay," I say a bit relieved. This is not personal. "Everyone was saying 'secondary explosions,' 'bombs planted inside.' I'm not surprised. They used bombs in '93 too. I don't remember ever hearing more about it, though. Even Claudius never mentions it. Granted he's a nuts and bolts man and pretty much sticks to his area of expertise."

My eyes focus on something beside the leather chair on a small table that I hadn't noticed before, a small black thing—a TV remote. I glance around me, and *there* on the wall behind me—where before an old yellowed French painting of a maritime battle had been, ochre sails and fog glowing with a quiet beauty in the fires of war—was a flat-screen TV. How I hate that man.

"They never tested," says Horatio.

"Who's they?" I ask, though my mind is focused on my mounting hatred for Claudius. I pick up the remote and place it on a high shelf behind some books. "Ha," I can't help but laugh, thinking about his frenzied search, missing half his favorite football game or talent show or whatever it is.

Horatio goes on, "FEMA, the FBI, the teams working on the reports."

"Never tested for explosives?"

"No, and they never actually investigated how the collapse happened." Horatio seems like my teacher again, tolerant of my distraction, confident that he can pull me into his subject.

"Claudius worked on that," I tell him.

"Claudius worked on a bolt as you say," Horatio goes on. "The report itself never investigated the causes of the collapses."

"I've seen the report—maybe I haven't read it, but at least I've weighed it in my hand. It must be here somewhere, in fact." I start scanning the shelves for it.

"I've read the report," says Horatio. He takes off his glasses and rubs his eyes liberally for a good long while before continuing tiredly in monotone. "Pages of analysis describing how plane and fire damage made the upper floors start to lean over. And then they say, *then the rest of the buildings fell down*, without explaining *how* that happened or what happened to all the steel and concrete."

"Another reason for me to hate that useless bureaucrat. They get into trouble for that? What did they do, spend the budget on champagne hot tubs in Vegas? I know they got $20 million to write that report. Not much compared to what was spent investigating Monica Lewinsky's laundry, but a good enough amount. Claudius certainly did well enough for himself."

Horatio frowns. "It wasn't on the news, but they weren't able to explain why those buildings came down like that. They couldn't. Not without testing the dust."

"Bad building design then?"

"They say the design was not the fault."

"They didn't offer a theory and test it? That's what they were paid to do. Bureaucrats couldn't possibly be *that* bad, even Claudius. I don't believe it."

"Why should you?"

"Because you're telling me so."

Horatio makes a half-crooked smile.

"How could they do something like this with everyone watching?" I ask somewhat dismissively, but Horatio remains patient.

"You lost your father. Were you watching?" he says, very gently. "Did you read the report? If not you or your mother, then who would?"

"I was just a little boy."

"Actually, there were families who tried, but the bureaucracy wore them out."

Horatio crosses the carpet and picks up his heavy canvas bag and begins to unpack its contents onto the coffee table. He shows me the copy of the towers report, a similar copy of which had, at one time, been lying desperately open on the dining room table, at the page where the introduction to Claudius's section appears. Then Horatio takes out a similarly bound report labeled "Building 7."

"You do know about this building? Damaged by North Tower debris. It was demolished at about five p.m. that day."

"I do remember seeing that. Home to the CIA and other nice folk. Just the CIA being the CIA. Maybe it had sensitive information or something. I figured the government has its reasons."

"This report claims office fires weakened a connection at a single column."

"To bring the whole thing straight down like that? Well now they're just being funny. You could tell it was a controlled demolition. I remember seeing it once on the news. Everybody said so at the time."

"They changed the story while you were looking the other way."

"That's weird. Why not just say, 'Screw you. We're the government. We're not going to tell you why we took it down'?"

"I don't know. Claudius might have some kind of answer."

"Hm," I consider. "I don't think it will be possible to speak to that snake."

"Who knows? Honestly, I don't."

"When did you find this out?"

"A little more than a year ago. I'm sorry I didn't tell you sooner. I wanted to make sure myself. So I had the tests replicated. It took awhile. Not all the sample is there," he says, nodding at the plastic bag on the table. "I took some of it, but I have that safe still too. I thought you might want to bury the rest of it."

"Bury it?" I pick up the bag, feel its gritty contents through the plastic. "Oh my god." There is more to this, I begin to realize, than the long-established fact of Claudius's incompetence. Something unspeakably rank and foul. "Let me have those reports. I'll read them now."

He takes out a folder with loose papers in it. "Here are the dust analyses. One from the US Geological Survey, one funded by Deutsche Bank, two from independent scientists in Utah and Copenhagen. And mine." He lays his report on top. "I haven't published it yet. You'd think I was trying to publish a paper on genetic cleansing. No one will look at it."

I stare vacantly at the homework assignments that my science teacher is piling up on my table. "It's that day all over again, Mr. Horatio. I feel attacked and helpless. The sky is black and the war has begun."

"Yes, I know. I'm so sorry Hamlet."

Chapter Eight
Alas, poor America

Hamlet alone in the tree house, holding a crumpled plastic bag.

Here I have the evidence. And yet, this is a thing harder to believe than Claudius's story, for which I had seen no proof, not a shred, nothing. I thought I knew. Now that I have this bag of dust, these reports, I couldn't be more uncertain if my father's ghost had been the one to come tell me, chill my marrow, blow hell's wind in my face, beg me, pathetically, to swear to take revenge.

The boards on which I walk move under my feet, and the stars overhead have rearranged and renamed themselves so that I can't get my bearings. Who killed my father? I thought I knew. Was it a bit of friendly fire, so to say, a small sacrifice, painful surely, but necessary, yes necessary, to get the lockdown going? Now I must sift through this grainy dust, rough and strange, like moondust, like nothing I have ever seen before, for answers. *He could be here.* A bit of him could be here in this dust, a tiny bit of each one of them could be here all mixed together indifferently with the gypsum and the polypropylene, just like they were in the first explosion, the big one, that primordial nothingness of nonbeing.

These last few days I have been up and down. Anger takes me rattling over tracks right through the barricades, and then despair finds me sitting engine cold with nothing but a bag of dust, and no one to talk to. My mother, she should be here with me now, not with that man. She should be in hell with me now, and she's not. We never mourned, Mother. We never really cried our eyes out. We moved on. We got by. We adjusted. We slipped into having fond memories.

They didn't even try, the cocky bastards. They didn't even try to estimate the mass or the kinetic energy. They didn't even measure the speed of the fall or look at what happened after the floors started to topple.

Here I hold in my hand the evidence that could stop wars. In this dust is the story, the index of our times, that if read—all one has to do is read (I say, voice cracking) (I am becoming pathetic, even I hate me)—all the murder and greed could be stopped. I think I've always hated them, hated the whole lot of them. I just thought they had nothing to do with me.

My dust is one among four samples, but mine is the best, says Horatio, the one that will hang them all. That's a funny world that assigns such a role to a small boy. I remember. I remember bending down and looking at it in a trance and scooping it up with my little hands and holding it loosely as if it were a live animal I was afraid to crush.

Oh my god it's not true! Everything everyone has said. It's all not true. They never explained it. They didn't even cover it up with a really good lie. They just said, *And then the buildings fell down; we don't really know why.* A little detail. Twenty million spent and not a dime on the real question: How did the buildings come down?

Not to mention, who or why.

I open the screen of my arboreal tower window to get a clear view of the cottage. Claudius's sedan is once again parked in the drive. Inside they two are at breakfast worrying about mad Hamlet who won't come down from his tree. For three days now I have read, drunk and fitfully slept in "a hateful, rotten, ugly world," I scream at them. For three days, I have kept to myself. I have eaten straight from the garden. I have spent my time scrolling through pages of debate and denial, obfuscation. Those criminals are insane. I can see it in the words they use, rigid and formulaic. Eccentrics, like me, are various, but all sociopaths are alike.

They use rhetoric. They attack the messenger not the message. They change the subject when they are asked to test the dust sample results. They appeal to their own authority, not evidence. They ridicule. They laugh at me, miserable son of a murdered father. And they say, in the calmest of tones, *like they really do believe it all*, that the most unlikely things are most likely. People hear the tone, and they go, "Ah well then okay. I believe that" and they don't stop to consider *what* was said. Why didn't they find his body? Answer me that? Because he wasn't crushed, stabbed by steel frames and pounded by concrete floors into a meaty pulp. He wasn't even roasted like a pig. He was incinerated, turned to ash, to moondust.

Someone would have talked, they say. That's enough to end the conversation. Someone would have talked. Who bothers to ask, *Did* someone talk? What agents were sent to the front like Bathsheba's husband? Were the people who would know in the tower, waiting for a meeting that never got started because the man who called the meeting was across the street watching?

Oh, my computer screen here has stories to tell. One has to know the magic words, "nano-thermite," "iron micropsheres," "open sesame," "elemental sulfur," but open up it does and says much. There he is, Claudius tiptoeing out the front door, barefoot, in his nappy cotton robe, probably stolen from a Hilton. He is wondering what that crazy scream was. Now Gertrude beckons him back in for more Nescafé or octopus ink, or whatever it is people like him drink in the morning. Is he a murderer, accessory to murder? Traitor? Impossible fool? But then, if he was given no dust or steel samples to study, how could he have known? He never went into the rubble to have a good look around for himself. He sat at his desk and waited until someone slid a paper under his nose to read. Traitor! No, worse than traitor, fool.

Can it be a great conspiracy, involving presidents and queens, the House of Saud, minor politicians, editors, newscasters, academics, liberals, and neo-cons and all their children, wives and dogs? Or is it all just a mindless robust system, members all in lockstep, not one of them in charge —not in any real way—all of it depending instead upon our herd instincts, our flocking tendencies. Just look at history. Can it be that a handful of men, a dozen at most, with well-crafted memos, can make a great thing happen? Nucleate the supercooled water, the crystal that spreads everywhere? Just the right suggestion, that catches on. Could they depend on W to play his part so well, as long as they kept him in the dark?

Conspiracy theorists can imagine it was all micromanaged either by One who is everywhere always or by countless intervening angels, demons and whatnot. I refuse to believe. I will not believe in an all-powerful Bilderberg being. I say it's all turned by the great wheel habit, seasoned with that dumb luck which is so good at preserving the status quo. One reporter repeats the first, and regularity spreads, crystallizing the official story. They check each other's stories every day. They report on reporters. They're repeaters, not reporters.

Oh heavens, have all the gatekeepers left their posts? Are they sleeping? Are they mad? Are they paid? Evil? Or is it just that they let only those in whom their nearest gatekeepers are also letting in? Watchtower Ninety-Four does just what Watchtowers Ninety-Two through Ninety-Seven do.

And so on.

My fingertips hurt. My scalp buzzes. I would like a good, hot bath. But what color is this postmodern theory that the public has? Assuming it has one. hThe incompetence of government is the only thing certain in the world, the only fact of nature indisputable. How ill-advised those activists were to choose the name "truth" for their campaign. That word is as out of fashion as the twin tower architecture that good old Mumford hated so much. What an aesthetic outrage, now down and destroyed.

Enter Rosencrantz and Guildenstern dressed in military camouflage.

"What's this? Hiding in the foliage?"

"We thought we would say good-bye, Hamlet."

"What news? Sudden decision!"

"Not really. Rosencrantz told you we signed up."

"You did? Well, I didn't hear it."

"We leave for training tomorrow," says Guildenstern, squeezing through the door and sitting himself down on the little low bench next to Rosencrantz. Their uniforms and new standard crew cuts make them now completely impossible to tell apart.

"Have to lose a few pounds," adds Rosencrantz laughing. "Guildenstern almost didn't make it in. Give us a few weeks in the desert. Will shed the weight like melted butter on hot corn."

They will not survive the desert. "Oh, that's bad news. Why would you want to do that? Don't you realize you could get killed over there? Or, at the very least, kill others who don't want killing?"

"The army takes care of you pretty good. We should get into tech school when we get back."

"How long?"

"Two years," they say in unison.

"That's an eternity in hell, and anyway, you'll come back all crazy. You'll scream in your sleep, and you'll rave on the street. Then the VA will pump you full of drugs to calm you down, which will just freak you out even more, and one day you'll wake up standing in the midst of twenty bodies with an automatic weapon in your hand."

"Hamlet, you don't know what you're talking about."

"I do, but only a little, I admit. I just spoke with my friend, Laertes, last week. You should talk to him, before you go. He has horrible stories to tell."

"War is never easy," says Rosencrantz.

"Oh, you buffoon, stop thinking in clichés. *This* war is wrong. Now is not the time to go risk your life for the government. We've been lied to."

"Oh, not more of that!" laughs Guildenstern with a knee-jerk reaction so quick it startles me.

"And the Kennedy assassination was the CIA," adds Rosencrantz. "The gullibility of conspiracy theorists amazes me. Do they think that Elvis is still alive and working in Walmart?"

"In the first place," says Guildenstern, "the WMD wasn't the real reason we went in. The point was to rout Saddam."

"Now with 9/11, that's all been gone over. They would have seen people coming in with that much explosive equipment. Someone would have talked."

I am shocked that they know something about this, whereas I knew nothing. *Someone would have talked.* I am upside-down now, with my mental pockets emptied. As a boy I would just let them take my coins, as I will do now. They chuckle soundlessly, bodies heaving and vibrating. They cannot imagine that I, out-of-touch Hamlet, might have some evidence in my sweaty palm. I gaze at my precious plastic bag. "People have talked," I say in a voice that sounds strangely without conviction.

"No planes hit the buildings, and it was all staged in Hollywood, like the moon landings. There is no limit to the lunacy of the tinfoil hat brigade."

I turn and look out the window. They have memorized the script. They can fill in the little bubbles on their standardized tests just well enough to get by.

"I've read a lot over the past few days. The Obama administration says that truthers suffer from 'media isolation.' " How true. I have not heard the *vox populi*. I've missed all the shows. As soon as the airlines were up and running again, Gertrude and I flew off to Lake Como for two months and took no news. "I missed that crucial televised period, in which Americans, brains flooded with oxytocin, were told the 'truth.' "

G & R have been silenced, for clearly, though I may be talking aloud, I do not speak to them. Looking out the window, I see clouds coagulating in the east under the risen sun, blushing pink with bruised shadows beneath them. A stand of silver leaf maples shivers like running crystal water, as the wind stirs them up and signals a change of weather. I brush a pile of dead insects that I notice have accumulated on the sill, moths mostly, a few wasps. Finally I ask, as if I were continuing the conversation, "What did you do those last weeks of September? Do you remember where you were, what you did and heard and how the news came to you? Or is it all a blur you no longer are able to separate from reality?"

They look at me like I'm babbling. I glance down at the reports that are lying on the floor. I could pick one up and turn to page 146 and show them where the government ends its own investigation before explaining the collapse. I could show them the copy of the letter Horatio gave me, in which they admit they never bothered to test for explosives. I could show them how key parts of the buildings were sprayed with "fire proofing" material in the summer of 2001, and how nano-thermite has a spray-on application. I could beg them to look at the science, to follow the money to the weapons and intelligence industries to which government has been outsourced, all at great taxpayer expense. I could show them copies of the reports in my hand, all dog-eared now and marked with notes. But I realize it won't matter, no more than it mattered when Gertrude tried to teach their parents about nutrition. "Facts don't matter," said the white-bearded sage in the grocery store aisle.

Rosencrantz, or is it Guildenstern, is picking bits of breakfast out of his teeth. They both recline, digesting their pancakes and sausage, enjoying the morning air.

Some herd instinct selected for over the millennia. Here am I, a wether cut off from the flock. I feel the terror in my blood. So this is how it will go. Even if I were big and bold and testicular, alone I could not fight a pack of wolves. I have even heard of a single domestic dog hounding an isolated elk for days, tiring him out, not letting him eat or stop for a drink, harassing him and harassing. The dog doesn't eat either, but he can go much longer without meat than the buck can go without grass. Finally, the noble beast goes down without a fight.

They will win, I realize. Those two, they will win.

Chapter Nine
Claudius in the Closet

How does the Claudian mind work? I wonder, as I watch him through the window at his desk, in what was my room. He turns on his computer and answers the password prompt. First letter is with left index finger. He is using just his left hand. Okay, there's one letter with his right.

"Who, who?" I call.

He jumps, peers out the window into the blank night, sees only his reflection and goes back to his computer. I have spent two nights watching him, hoping that he'll show some sign of the state of his soul. Guilty? Stupid? Or somewhere in between?

The Bard lets us glimpse Claudius's thoughts when he prays in his closet, confessing his guilt. Poor ignorant Hamlet, who is stepping lightly behind, comes too late. He misses the chance to verify the ghost's revelations. Hamlet may have seen the ghost with his own eyes and heard him with his own ears, but empiricism doesn't count against the supernatural. It may be a lying devil.

My bare feet are cold, but I cannot pull myself away from my watch. As much as I trust transmission electron microscopy, a detailed confession would be nice, like chicken soup. If only I could hear his thoughts in soliloquy. Would he go on like an engineer thinking of bolts and steel, clockwork, levers? Or does he have some rudimentary feelings, such as rodents have or dogs?

Shall I tap into his phone lines, read his e-mails, reconstitute his shreddings?

The hour is late and coyotes laugh wildly on the rail trail. They come down from the north in packs when the fall starts to come on. To bed.

Exit Hamlet.

Sometime earlier in 2005.
Enter Claudius.

Claudius is at his desk in Gaithersburg poring over his assignment to test the stress level of bolt #93798. He met Gertrude one month ago yesterday, and he has seen her ten times, including three recent nights in a row.

It is hard for him to concentrate. He has done many tests at different temps, from slight to extreme. He isn't allowed to use known data, or even common sense, to predict what the very predictable type of bolt, like #93798, will do at a given temperature. He actually has to run the experiments, filling up drives of data. Claudius has subjected this bolt to unrealistic extremes, and always his boring, but very neat, reports report the same, very unsurprising results. He is lucky that he can afford to be distracted right now.

His report is very thorough but seems incoherent, even insane, because he isn't sure of the goal. He doesn't understand what they want from him. They keep asking for more and more test runs. He can't remember how many hours he has clocked watching yet another #93798 bravely endure the furnace. Turning up the heat, adding more weight/stress until poor #93798 begins to show signs of fatigue at hour nineteen. Still not enough. He must drive it to its limits faster.

In the past, Claudius worked on span twist and stress. It was early 2000 that he switched to bolts and heat. He's got a coffee ring on the printouts, followed by several shadow rings. At least he can tell this report from the last one, which said essentially the same thing about another instance of #93798. Each of its predecessors has been subjected to a similar battery of tests. All this is turning him into a bore. What kind of small talk can he make with Gertrude about work these days? And she believes he is doing something important because of the nature of the investigation. He doesn't have the heart to tell her that his part, so far at least, seems utterly pointless. He must somehow pretend that he still thinks he's making a small contribution to a project of enormous import.

Last night Gertrude had probably smelled his gas. But he cleverly mentioned the brussels sprouts to implicate them instead. He wasn't sure if it had worked, but he pretended it had, and she either pretended too or hadn't noticed. Either way, he was relieved. Another #93798 is in the furnace. This time his assignment is to get it to the breaking point, not by adding more heat or more time, only stress. All right, more stress. At least he didn't have to imagine where the stress was supposed to come from. Some other hack like himself, a few floors up or down, is working on that part of the problem, probably. He hopes that *he* is just as bored as he is, disinterested, ready to file, sign and move the hell on.

She had stayed over at his apartment and she had cooked for him. He actually preferred eating out; that way you can release some gas on the walk home. A walk after dinner makes sense. He'll suggest it next time they stay in.

Yesterday the team had gathered on the lawn for the group photo. It was to go on the website and in the report. His comb-over had flipped on and off in the wind. Knowing that he was going to be photographed, he had used Gertrude's hairspray to fix the top as a solid mass. Seems every time you try to prevent something, you only make it worse. It would have been better if the long hairs had just been left to scatter in the wind. That would have been better than the flip-flop of the hair mat unit. Probably the photographer caught it when it was flipped open. He tried to comb his fingers through it to break it up, but the stuff held.

Luckily he won't have to work on the Building Seven report. He got out of that one. Poor Osric wasn't able to make the excuses in exactly the right way. Rewards tempting, but what a can of worms. Sometimes money just isn't enough. Some devilry going on there. No thanks. The whole thing is politicized; that is the problem. When that happens, you throw mountains of data at the media until they become so bored they forget why they were ever interested. Everybody here knows it was the insurance. Repairing a building with that kind of damage is expensive. More economical to take it down, and already the air was full of toxins, so what did it matter if they did it quick and dirty?

It's all too complex. A mountain of selfish motives intermingled with more or less good will. Who is he to try to disentangle the ethics? One thing is clear: it is best to do what is asked of him. Luckily no lying is needed. He just has to torture some poor bolt beyond all reason. What's the harm in that? And who cares if it seems unnecessary and bad science to go on in this way? Most people will just accept that science is dull. That's how you got it in school, just endless exercises without any clear objective other than to do as you are told, and if you do that, you are good boys and girls. His part is nothing. Another #93798 is in the furnace. A few Afghani and Iraqi boys are killed, but they would have grown up to be terrorists anyway. The soldier's part is nothing. He does what is asked of him, and we need war. You make war because that is what pays. By doing what he's told, he gets his Gertrude. Another #93798 is in the furnace. This time the stress and heat make it break at the third hour. That will do.

Had he bored Gertrude, or more to the point, had she made a comment about his balding pate? He concentrated on the bit of portuguese roll between his eyetooth and molar, inaccessible by tongue. Nail no help either. Right now that bit of starch was more on his mind than the condition of the bolt. At this point, he could run the experiment unconsciously, as well as he could operate his coffeemaker. Tomorrow they would ask for another run, "to be really thorough." It was thorough all right. That bolt has seen the improbable furnace of hell and perseveres until it finally snaps on cue. More heat, less stress, less heat and more stress, more time, less time. More time, less heat and or stress. The manufacturer published a look-up table showing all the results that he was "researching." But what the hell, to be thorough was the thing.

Claudius took some comfort deciding that Gertrude should not see the pictures. Probably she would not read the report. No one would. He did not plan on reading the other parts of it. The thing, as a whole, would be nothing but a fermented blend of preconception and irrelevance.

When the report comes out, Claudius leaves it on Gertrude's kitchen table. She glances at the table of contents, turns to his chapter, scans it, and says she would read it later. "I'm so grateful to you for doing this work." He never sees her sitting down reading it. Probably she never got around to it. Finally, after two weeks, he takes the heavy bound copy and puts it away in his office drawer. They never speak of it again. Three years later, Gertrude is his wife.

Chapter Ten
Lord of Misrule

September 18, 2009. Gertrude's thin voice calls up to me in my tree house. "Hamlet, are you there?"

They have been back days now. Still I have not shown myself. I stole in for a shower this morning when I saw that they had gone out. I left traces, dirty footprints and wet towels on the bathroom floor, to re-mark my territory.

"Hamlet, are you there?"

"You who," calls back my disembodied soul. "Here I am."

She climbs inside looking around at my scattered papers and blankets. "Hamlet," she says, irritated, as if I were a slovenly child who won't keep his room clean. "You have to try to get along with Claudius at some point."

"Right now may not be exactly the best time."

"Why, what's going on now, I mean, other than my marriage?"

I widen my eyes at her, but say nothing.

"Hamlet, why don't you come for dinner tonight. I'm making lamb."

"Plutomutton," I say, nodding.

"Hamlet," she whines. "Poor Pluto, I know. But it's just a shank I took out of the freezer. I don't know which one. I don't keep track."

"That's best. We don't like to eat our friends."

"Polonius, Laertes, and Ophelia are all coming too, so maybe that's less awkward for everybody."

When I arrive they are all already at table, Claudius, who has squeezed himself into that smelly old sweater again, at the head (hubris!) across from his wife, my mother. Gertrude has had her sleeves rolled up, preparing the food. She straightens them and buttons her cuffs before putting her napkin in her lap. Ophelia sits by her father with her brother across from her. My view of Ophelia will be catty-corner through the candlesticks. She has set by her emo girl costume and is wearing a flattering navy dress, with long sleeves and a modest neckline. Her hair has been carefully curled with some hot device into a dozen or so vertical copper coils. It's pretty, and reminds me of Eve's spring traps. I have the urge to mess it all up with both hands. Her brother has donned civilian clothes, grey slacks and a button-down, beautifully tailored for wide neck and bulging biceps. They look like a couple on a date, those two. As I'm barefoot, in jeans and an old T-shirt, Gertrude feels compelled to make excuses for my appearance. "He's been camping out in the tree house," she explains completely unnecessarily.

After the greetings and inquiries after everyone's health have been taken care of, I sit down gloomily with Polonius in front of me. He looks pitifully thin. The window backlights his papery ears, which, I've noticed over the years, are growing like mushrooms. With a slight Parkinson's tremble, he brings a glass of water to his mouth, stretches out a thin prehensile upper lip and makes a slurping noise that turns Gertrude's head. She immediately pretends not to have heard. I wonder how Ophelia is with the sounds he makes at feeding time. Claudius, to my right, passes me the salad bowl with hairy hand. I do not look at his face.

"I read in the paper that Rosencrantz and Guildenstern joined the army," says Gertrude cheerily.

"It's true," I reply darkly, "I bade them farewell already."

"Maybe it will be good for them, teach them some discipline," quips Polonius.

"Very likely," adds Laertes, looking at me.

"Mom, you'll never guess who I ran into at the Farmers' Market when you were away," I say. "My old grade school science teacher, Mr. Horatio." I'd had no intention of bringing this up, but the news popped out of me like a demon.

"Mr. Horatio. I remember him, a good-looking fellow. Your father liked him. I remember he said so. I always thought he was gay. Is he?"

"Probably," I reply icily.

Polonius emits a "tsk-tsk."

Ophelia sighs at her father.

"So what did he have to say? Why is he up in Amenia?"

"Forgot to ask. I haven't seen him since the—since September 11th. You do remember that day? He found me by the bridge and brought me home?"

Gertrude lowers her face. "I remember he did that," she says in a solemn, almost prayerful tone.

"He said there were explosives planted in the buildings," I bring out with as much indifference as I can muster. Perhaps I am actually hopeful that my friends and mother will take my news seriously, ask me questions, have a good debate, get to the bottom of things.

Polonius makes another, more disgusted, "tsk-tsking" noise.

"Oh, come on now, Hamlet," snaps Claudius. "That's all been gone over."

Gertrude shrinks. Laertes and Ophelia are either too busy filling their plates or, out of politeness, take no notice of the ape presiding at the head of the table.

"I know you studied your bolt, Uncle. Did you read the rest of the report?" I ask awkwardly. "Horatio says you and your friends didn't test for explosives."

He puts his fork down noisily. "Did I *read* the rest of the report? *Of course* I read the report. I helped *write it* for Christ's sake." Now Claudius has everyone's attention. An audible silence follows while he angrily slices his meat, stabs a morsel, then bites it off his fork (sound of teeth on metal) and chomps noisily, breathing through his mouth.

Gertrude asks, obviously trying to deflect attention away from my impolitic remark, "You helped write the whole report?"

Claudius, slightly annoyed, answers curtly, "My part. We did not influence each other's work. More objective that way."

"I don't think you read it," I say, tearing a bite off my hard roll.

"Don't be silly Hamlet. I read the damn report. Every section was every bit as thorough as mine. There was a lot of data, a lot of detail. Most of us ran our experiments multiple times. It's all there. Steel may not melt, but it weakens in the temperatures that were present. That's what we found."

"I'm afraid your idea isn't very original. Iron Age man beat you to it," I say, making my mother wince. "Why did the steel that wasn't hot give like that?"

My mother interrupts to offer Polonius and family further condiments. Her plan doesn't work though: Claudius has taken the bait and starts thrashing with it.

"I did what I was asked to do. It's not my fault that people weren't satisfied with the obvious. Planes hit the buildings: the buildings collapsed."

"*Post hoc ergo propter hoc?*" I ask, starting to feel confident that I have taken the high ground.

Then Laertes breaks in. "He's right," he says, addressing me with a hint of condescension. "There is no evidence of explosives. Conspiracy theorists just distract everyone from the real issues."

I turn to my left to look at him. I feel blood rise to my cheeks, and I can think of no reply.

Gertrude is rearranging her water glass and soupspoon, having now completely failed to keep the dinner conversation mild. Polonius groans softly. He clearly doesn't want to hear more about the "real issues."

"That's true," says Ophelia. "What's so laughable about conspiracy theories," she goes on, in a manner I've heard her use on her inferiors, "is the idea that a bunch of bureaucrats could pull off something like that. I'm sorry Claudius. No offense. I was just—".

"None taken," says Claudius gloomily.

"Some people find comfort in conspiracy theories. It's frightening to think that the world's best military just wasn't in control that day," says Laertes.

"I know what you mean, Laertes," says Gertrude, no doubt relieved that a soft-footed consensus is now making the rounds at her table.

"I'm not saying that our government is above criticism, far from it," continues Laertes, composed, polite, confident, and a tiny bit patronizing, icing on the cake of his effective dinner table demeanor. "I just think a lot of time has been wasted on this topic. What we really ought to be investigating are the lies that sent us to Iraq."

Polonius sighs.

Adrenaline runs to my fingertips and scalp, as if I've just taken a misstep on the path. I sit quietly, allowing dishes to be passed and food-related remarks to be made around me. Summarily rebuffed at my own table, by Laertes and Ophelia too, as if I were a stupid child. They make light of it. I have played the clown so long they can't imagine I have feelings.

Laertes eats his meat heartily. He still has an appetite, medication or not. Ophelia is slicing her meat into minuscule bites. It hadn't been easy for me to draw out my little nugget about Horatio.

Coughing into his napkin, Polonius signals he is going to orate. "A few months ago," he announces, "I heard about a low-budget documentary, a PowerPoint presentation, in fact, that was produced by an organization *known as* 'Architects and Steel Workers for 9/11 Truth,' something like that, who claimed to offer 'evidence,'" drawing quotes in the air with knife and fork, "that the World Trade Center high-rises were destroyed not by fire and damage, but by 'explosive-controlled demolitions.'" Quotes flutter in the air again.

"In other words, they claim *someone* wired these buildings with explosives intending to bring them down after the planes hit them, and this has been covered up by the government, the 9/11 Commission and the mainstream media," dramatic pause. "*I* find the idea of a government conspiracy preposterous and simply beyond belief."

Ophelia and Laertes, mouths full, make concurring noises.

Polonius adds, "If they decided they didn't need to test for explosives, they probably had good reason. That's all you need to know."

"Authority trumps evidence? Sounds like good old-fashioned Scholasticism," I say. Laertes and Ophelia look at me with mild curiosity.

"Oh, I don't know about *that,*" replies Polonius a little huffily. "The most widely cited dismantling of this theme came in *Popular Mechanics* magazine in 2005, with a follow-up in 2007. My layman's views, for what they are worth, have never changed."

"*Popular Mechanics* is to engineering what *Reader's Digest* is to literature. Dentists and chiropractors subscribe," I mumble.

"What Hamlet?" asks Ophelia.

"Precisely, a very respectable publication. You know *The 9/11 Commission Report* was a finalist in the National Book Award! Even its literary merits were recognized. So very clear and detailed in its descriptions, it reads like a first-rate docudrama, truly. Mostly, I admire its objectivity, reporting exact times and giving names—they got everything straight from those guys in Gitmo, and I mean everything. Very reliable information. I also appreciate the one powerful moment the authors wax poetic, 'The building collapsed into itself, causing a ferocious windstorm and creating a massive debris cloud.' Now that's literature. The entire collapse analysis takes as much time to read as it did for the buildings to fall." Polonius, assuming a thinking pose, reflects, "How poetic, really.

"The building collapsed
into itself,
causing
a ferocious
windstorm
and creating a
massive
debris
cloud.

"There's even a staccato effect that mirrors the pancaking at each floor: bump, bump bump. The report was an instant *best seller,* you know, unusual for a document written by committee. But its popularity is owed mostly to a spare, riveting narrative of the shocking events on September 11th, 2001." Polonius turns his attention back to his plate and goes to cutting, as if he is interested in, and expects, no response.

"I could not read that report," says Gertrude, evidently disturbed by Polonius's taste in poetry.

"Horatio says the pancake theory was ruled out: the upper floors accelerated through the lower ones." As I speak, I'm conscious that my voice does not sound the way I want it to. It wavers, pathetically, as if with stage fright. Can Ophelia hear it? I wonder, but I go on. "Claudius's friends admitted they were never able to explain the collapses, even though that's what they were supposed to do."

Ophelia looks at me. Her brows are just slightly raised. Then the corners of her mouth curl into a half smile, a look of amused surprise.

Before Claudius can respond, Polonius answers. "Hm, well still it's good writing. I wouldn't change it," he decides.

"Too many people asleep at the switch, they found. Incompetence is a terrible thing, but even the best have a bad day every once in a while.   Tragical-comical-historical, I should say."

"Tragical-comical-fantastical, I should say," I mumble.

"Hamlet!" whispers Gertrude.

"He can't hear me, Mother," I mouth at Gertrude. "Deaf."

Ophelia glares at me. I blink at her three times.

"You lost your father. Your friend should have considered that before trying to bring dishonor on his death," says Claudius.

"My father dishonored?" I say, quietly enraged.

"Oh, but these conspiracy theorists get equal time," says Polonius extending a hand to subdue me. "That's what democracy is all about, tolerating even the worst of society. Our First Amendment protects speech of even this kind. I think that's a good thing, and the truth 'expert' clearly has as much right to speak as a Klansman does."

Gertrude is mute.

"What is it to be 'wrong' or 'right'? We cannot say," continues Polonius.

"Science can't explain everything," says Ophelia, my Ophelia, as if buildings fall in Heisenberg's world not Newton's. Oh, my Ophelia.

"The best lesson science teaches us," continues Polonius, "is humility. That is what those truthers need to learn."

The blood in my head is pounding and my thoughts swim. Polonius goes on for a while, but I cannot listen to him anymore.

Then my cell begins to chime, which Polonius appears not to hear, as he keeps talking. I slip my phone out of my pocket and Gertrude shoots me a look. Phones at the table are forbidden.

I turn away from the table and whisper down into the phone. "Hello Man. In town again?"

"I want to pick you up. There's a party I want to take you to," says Horatio.

"Party where? Now?"

"In Poland, not far from you."

"I know Poland."

"Ten minutes?"

"See you then. I'm having dinner at the house now. I'll come out."

"Mine will be the car with one headlight."

I put my phone away and smile at my mother. "Excuse me."

"So, my conclusion is," Polonius goes on, "that I trust better the government's honest admission that they could not explain everything than those who pretend to know what happened by looking at dust samples and steel and video records and temperature readings and so forth."

Everyone is silent around the table.

"And why push them, huh?" I say, pushing back from the table and standing up. "Who needs a court to determine evidence when we have trustworthy intelligence contractors telling us all we need to know? Nasty business the whole thing. Better to move on, look forward, not back. Pluto was delicious by the way, Mother. You did a great job with the seasoning."

Ophelia frowns at her plate.

Horatio puts his face in his hands and rubs up and down vigorously, moaning. "Hamlet, I thought I warned you to stay in the closet." He puts his car in gear, circles round and heads back down the driveway. "Being for 9/11 truth in 2009 is like being for multiracial gay marriage in 1950. Don't bring it up with your friends at dinner."

"Oops," I say like a dope.

"You'll just get angry when they brush you off with some stupid notion that it is *impossible* to plant explosives without anyone noticing, or that there is *no motive,* or that there is no point in testing for explosives."

"I think I'm starting to get the idea," I say, staring ahead into the dark road, Horatio's single headlight leading the way. A full moon hangs, yellow and massive, in the center of the road, and we drive straight toward it. "Thanks to you, I no longer have a shared reality that is the basis for public discourse and polite conversation." I turn to him. He nods at the road.

"It's not just the yahoos who will hate me now," I say, after a long while of meditating upon the interrupted yellow line shooting past us on the long straight road. "I must relinquish my seat at the table with the highbrow, the degreed, *New York Times* subscribers, the fit and traveled, that community of well-intended liberals—with whom I share reading lists and favorite subtitled films." I take a deep sigh. "It's a horrible thing to be among the politically despised."

We are quiet for a long while. I roll down the window and smell Chinese food. Horatio says it's his car, runs on used cooking oil.

"There's plenty of it in the city. I may have to buy some fuel at the grocery store here."

I think once more how he is so like Gertrude. If only she could have found someone like him. "Why did they do it?"

"I don't know. Look at history. Take a guess. To funnel more money to military and intelligence contractors, so they can better control politics?"

"I don't know what to think anymore, Horatio. The world is upside down."

"It's no good to say, 'I'm not crazy' if they think you are," he says.

"How about claiming to be crazy?"

"Only a crazy person would claim to be crazy," says Horatio.

"I thought it worked by reverse logic. Say you're crazy and people think you're too self-aware to be crazy."

"Used to be true. Now you don't say you're crazy. You get a prescription."

"Otherwise you're crazy?"

"Something like that."

"So where are we going, exactly?" I ask.

"To have fun."

"Ha," I say, doubtful.

"There're a lot of us, everywhere, all over the country. I'm part of a group in Brooklyn," he says comically. "I found this one online. It turns out I already know some of the people who run it."

"Run it? Run what?"

"A political group without a platform, demands or goals. You'll see. You'll get it. Some of us tried passing out fliers once, but that sucks."

"What do you do then?"

"Wait for the other shoe to drop. It's a costume party, by the way. I brought a mask for you."

Horatio hands me a Cinderella mask with golden curls. Her pink lips have a vaguely obscene small hole in the center of the plastic and her pupils are deadly vacant. "Do I have the gown to go with it?"

"You bet. Look in the box."

In the backseat of his car I find the box to match the mask. Inside is a girl's XXL princess costume, an old-fashioned thing kids used to wear in the 1970s. I squeeze my arms through—the fabric splits a little—and tie it, as well as I can, in the back. "A little tight in the pits."

"Sorry I couldn't find glass slippers, but I did find some enormous leather pumps."

"What are you?" I ask.

"The prince, of course." Horatio shows me the complementary mask, with smarmy smile, also blond. "I found a thrift shop."

Horatio has also brought some hard cider. I drink less than half a bottle on the way, but my head soon starts feeling fuzzy. To think the Quakers used to have it for breakfast. We drive north of Poland a mile or two and then turn off into a farm complex, where an enormous Dutch barn is lighted and alive with music. It is almost eerie the way the thing is so well organized, so far off in the country, so deep in the otherwise quiet night. The air is warm, and the supermoon now douses the field in intoxicating blue light. The car rocks back and forth over the rutted dirt road, and we drive slowly forward. Horatio puts on his mask. I do the same. There are some shadowy figures roaming in the field. A group of six or seven overtake our car and walk alongside. At first I think they're naked apes, then I realize their brown bodies are painted with mud, and they're wearing hides over their shoulders. Their necks are level with the top of the window. I crouch down to have a look at their faces. I see animal skulls where their heads should be. The leader hurries out in front of the car wearing dark fleece and a skull with Plutolike black curly horns.

"Uh, what is this?" I ask.

As we near the barn, a man in a Guy Fawkes mask swings a flashlight in the direction of a row of cars parked in the field. We park next to an old pickup. Mr. Fawkes bends down to Horatio's window. He says something unintelligible, and Horatio answers in the affirmative. They shake hands when we get out of the car. I try on my new shoes. They fit, but I can't walk in them. Horatio lets me leave them in the car, and I make do with my Converses.

Coming and going over the field and into the barn, we see more people in costumes, a man in a bodysuit of grey fur and a coyote's head, a Rockette on stilts, a lap dog weaving in and out of her steps barking frantically, and seven silver-haired men dressed in fox-hunting costumes, tweed jackets, beige riding breeches with beautiful soft brown leather boots, crisp white cravats stuck with golden pins—the very *seven lords a leaping*. There is an Alexander Hamilton, the image of his ten-dollar portrait, dozens more in animal skull masks, three Gandhis and one Jesus, maybe a saint or two. The barn door opens, and hundreds of people already are inside.

"It looks like the whole village has turned out," I say.

The drafty barn smells of fresh hay. Wind is coming through cracks in the siding. On a stage at the back of the barn, under the hayloft, twenty or so people, in various states of undress, sit in a drum circle. In the center of the circle sits a very large person wearing nothing but a skirt and a pig mask, whether male or female it is hard to tell, the hairless rolls of fat suggest bosoms.

"The Lord of Misrule," says Horatio. "Every year they find one lucky guest to be king for the day. Everyone has to obey his command, which traditionally is just eat, drink, and be merry."

"What is the basis for election?"

"Actually—don't tell the lord this—the title is conferred on the one who seems least deserving of power and authority. The best way to keep an eye on him is to put him at the center."

"That's a man?" I ask.

Horatio squints at the pig figure and nods. "This is theater. We don't want anyone to take us seriously," Horatio adds, looking grim. "We're here to enjoy the harvest."

We find our way to a dining area, with rows of picnic tables covered with dishes. "It's a potluck," Horatio explains. "We should have brought something but I told the guy at the entrance who you were, and we got in free."

"Who I am?"

"The boy who collected the dust sample," he says simply.

My mouth drops open.

"You're famous." He adds, "Sort of."

"Like Harry Potter?"

Horatio laughs. "And he-who-shall-not-be-named cannot be named because no one will ever know, and there's no point in trying to find out."

Horatio says he hasn't eaten yet and fills a plate for himself from trays of lentils, kale, and "chic" peas. Gertrude would approve. A bear makes room for us at a table, and we put up our masks to talk. I ask Horatio if everyone here is a truther.

"Guy Fawkes was," says Horatio. "A lot of them probably are. We don't talk about it much anymore. We can't plan anything without their knowing about it and shutting it down."

Our wobbly table shifts when two hobbits sitting across from us get up to leave. Horatio and I have to hold on to our Mason jars filled with hard cider that the bear has brought us. A slim beautiful black woman in a blue leotard sits next to Horatio and starts making small talk. I recede into my own shell, glancing nervously around me.

I wonder if they are talking about it. I wonder how Horatio could talk about anything else. I would like to ask the bear if he knows, but I don't dare. I feel shy and awkward.

It's all so strange. For days now I've been swimming in a new unreality in which every occasion relates my thoughts back to the tragedy of the Prince of Denmark. I cannot get away from it. I cannot relax, or even worry about what used to be important, like Ophelia. I can't run through my list of things to do, mend a fence, clip a ewe's hoof, without coming back to that damn bag of dust, those reports, that bureaucrat, *that damn ghost telling me to take revenge*. It's all relevant now to one thing. It's as if I'm lost at night in a Parisian neighborhood and the streets keep leading me back to the same churchyard. I cannot get away from it. If I could only walk straight, but no, the streets curve and wind.

It seems odd that the rest of the world goes forward the way it used to. People in Amenia get up and go to work; they watch TV and pay taxes. They vote and they pee and poop, and they just go on. Meanwhile communications are filtered and reviewed. Everyone is watched and monitored, whistleblowers stopped before they can even pucker. Protests foiled. Lists made. Dissidents jailed. Politicians controlled by blackmail at least as much as bribes, controlled by the great all-seeing intelligence contractors, whose lapdog the NSA, does their bidding, not the other way around.

I am a hapless hero in a sci-fi dystopia, beginning to suspect there is an outside, beyond the stage set, of which he has never dreamed. In a way, of course, I'm shocked to find out this has happened, shocked to realize so many other people already know, even more shocked to think so many more don't know. And in some ways, too, I think I've always known.

"Like me," says Horatio cleaning the last of his plate (the lovely lady is gone), "you will make new friends among the foreclosed, the uninsured, college debt slaves, Greens and Libertarians, secessionists, Constitutionalists, Ebayers, veterans and antiwar protesters, YouTubers, raw milk drinkers, organic farmers, open-sourcers, anarchists, hemp growers, Internet freedom fighters, and hacktivists—localvores of all kinds."

"These are the people from the co-op with their own currency?"

"How to have a revolution without violence, without protests or rallies, without trials or new laws or elections. All we have to do is stop consuming their stuff. They will be their own undoing."

I see a kind of natural wisdom here, as I look around me at the spectacle. They don't want power, or pretend to know how to change things, they have no plans for bringing down the system themselves. They exist merely to provide the ritual element with their drumming, celebrating some natural cycle of death and rebirth.

I notice the pig man in the drum circle struggles to his feet. Clearly drunk, he can barely get down the steps leading from the stage to the plywood dance floor. I watch him make his way toward the restrooms, and I realize his rocking gait is familiar.

"That," I say to Horatio, "is Carlyle Hogg. A spy."

"He won't remember anything tomorrow."

As Hogg lumbers past us I mask myself. His bloodshot eyes peek through his mask at me, but I see no recognition in his beady pig eyes. Horatio grabs my arm and leads me to the stage to join the drum circle.

Horatio drops me off, late, after midnight, and I sit swinging in my hammock reflecting, staring up at the roof beams that the old cottonwood has slowly enveloped over the years. It's incomprehensible to someone like Carlyle Hogg that there is no information to discover, that they don't have a plan, that there is not a leader among them willing, or even able, to try to shape a mob into a political power, even less easy for Gertrude to understand methinks. She always has a plan for improvement.

This is a new way to go. I like it. Give the bastards enough rope to hang themselves with, and the mad chorus will just explain what's going on as it happens.

I remember I was disappointed when Faust, with all the power granted him by Mephistopheles, used his gifts to play disrespectful pranks on the pope and run around like a fool. How naive I was. Wise Goethe, he must have known. So now Anonymous replaces the Department of Justice's website with a video game. It's like farting in their faces. Hopelessness turns into a kind of giddiness.

Violence?

Not this time, I'm afraid. The mob seems to have subverted its urge, its right, to be angry.

There is something more powerful. The criminals know we know. They know we know they know. It's a standoff, an intellectual siege. We wait and we mind what we eat.

The wind has picked up and ribbons of clouds fly past the moon. I hear a bleating, a little far away and very dim, but very anxious. Someone has lost her flock. I open the door, and the wind, turning violent, grabs the door from my grasp and whacks it against the tree house. The bleating is louder now and more insistent. In my pocket I find my phone and open it for its light. As I run barefoot down the gravel path toward the pasture, a warm rain begins. I hear the ewe plainly now, though I cannot see her. The others are lying in the pasture near the barn looking vaguely interested in my approach, slightly suspicious of my blue light. They hurry to their feet as I come nearer and run away from me toward the back of the barn. I open the barn door. The bleating goes on. I turn around and around, but I cannot find her. The rain comes in torrents now, and the flock comes timidly from the back of the barn, and, one by one, they dart inside out of the downpour.

Then I see her. It's the little one born late this year, on Easter day, her long curly wool all tangled in raspberry brambles. She panics as I get near and tries to bolt away and becomes even more trapped. I wrap my arms around her gamey-smelling soft body and hold her firm. She goes limp, the way sheep do when they are frightened. The razor-like brambles cut my wrists, the rain comes down, and I fumble with my phone trying to use the light, while at the same time shielding it from the rain. I see the problem: an old bit of rusty barbed wire is in the mix, wrapped around her delicate little leg. There are always bits of old garbage turning up in the pasture—no matter how many times I comb it in winter —old glass, nails and other hazards. The carelessness of others, now decades old, still does its harm. Finally, I get her free.

"You know what? I think I'll go mad, Horatio," I say addressing Easter who, though free, lies on the ground staring at me in terror. "When the world is crazy then it is the sane ones who appear to have lost their wits. Crazy it is then. Hysteria, be thou my sanity."

Easter realizes she is free and scrambles to her feet and joins the others in the barn.

"From this time forth,   my thoughts be hysterical, or be nothing worth!"

Exit.

Act III

Chapter Eleven
The Straw Trick

September 19, 2009.

"Hamlet!" Ophelia jumps when I overtake her on the rail trail.

"Run with me fair Ophelia. I don't want my heart rate to go down."

"I'm not wearing the right shoes."

"I'm surprised to see you here," I say breathlessly, wiping sweat from my nose. "Perhaps you hoped to meet me? It is well known that I take exercise here."

She frowns at my diction, whose allusiveness eludes her.

"Didn't you see my father? You just passed him on the bench."

"There was some geezer said hello to me just now, but I didn't take him in."

"He turned his ankle or something. We were out for a walk together. I'm going back for the car now." She holds up a set of keys.

"Well come on then, let's run to your car together," I say, still jogging, now more or less in place.

"These aren't running shoes."

I cock my head at her thick-soled boots. "Give me the keys, I'll get the car. You stay with your father."

She keeps at her pace. "I'll just go. He's all right. He's just old and fussy."

"Piggyback then," I say, squatting down in front of her legs and nudging myself between them.

"Hamlet," she says laughing. Glancing back in her father's direction, she brushes off her skirt. "Stop it," she says with a big smile. Then with a change of expression, she adds, "I'm too heavy."

"You're just the right size, fair Ophelia." This does not bring back her smile. Stupidly I add, "I liked your natural hair color. It went with your complexion."

"Red goes with my personality," she says defensively and automatically, as if she says this often.

"Does it? You see, I didn't know that, but you were much younger then."

"I have gotten older, but now I'm too young."

I try to keep my heart rate up by bringing my knees up higher as I jog in place. "These three years I've always pictured you with chestnut hair, wearing your beloved deep maroon dress that brought out your eyes."

"I don't remember a maroon dress." She keeps her gaze on the trail before her.

"Don't remember? How could you forget? You wore it every day. You used to be late all the time because 'the dress' was in the dryer. Let me tell you how lovely that dress was, if you don't remember. You should have a copy made, adjusted for your new size, at the tailor in Poland."

"There's a tailor in Poland?" she says in a kind of automated reply, as if she's not really listening.

"There is a tailor. His name is Bob. He can help you find the perfect shades, the perfect textures, if he's not too drunk."

"I like this blue."

"It's okay. But sky blue is rather too nice, isn't it? All about Easter and infantilism. Not that people consciously process all that, but it's the submerged part of their brains that whips the pony." I'm still doing my high knees. "As long as it isn't grass or Irish, green is more complicated than blue. Sea green, tornado green, lichen, these are some of your best colors. You can wear light blue sometimes, but only when you're pretending that you don't want people to take you seriously."

"You've given this some thought," she says without looking at me.

"You must never wear synthetics, and tell Bob to cut on the bias." I go on, although she is clearly not listening. "There'll be waste, but it's worth it for the drape. He can make you the eight to ten dresses you need, and you can throw the rest away."

"Throw them away?" she whines, glancing at me for a moment, then forcing herself to look straight ahead.

"Give them away, especially that one Ophelia. It may be fashionable to drop the waist, but it makes your legs look short. You girls fail to consider the body you got from nature, and you dress it up according to the fashion. You buy off the rack, you buy a lot and you buy often and you're always unhappy, because it's never the dress made just for you." I stop to get my breath. "Discrimination is out of style, what a shame. You need the *best* things, not *a lot* of things. You can afford to discriminate, Ophelia. You're rich. It's the one good thing rich people can do with their money. You can buy *fine* things, so that the poor workers can be artisans not sweatshop slaves. Now the tailor will tell you your body wants a high-waisted dress."

"Hamlet that's rude," she says, eyes filling to the rims.

Guilt jabs my calloused heart. I don't know why I want to be so nasty to her. I put on a kinder expression, stop, take her by her soft round shoulders, and look her in the eye. My heart's mood follows my mask's, and I say gently, "That lovely little prune-colored dress had a high waist. The hem hit right above your peek-a-boo knees. The sleeves were short and slightly gathered. The neckline was low and showed your matte white skin. My heart rate is up a little, Ophelia."

"Hamlet! You're sweaty."

"And mad as a corkscrew." I hold her shoulders tight and try to kiss her, but she pulls back.

"I promised my father that I wouldn't see you."

"Promised your father?"

"Yes. You're hurting my neck."

"There, I've let go. I did love you once."

"I believed it once."

"It's our generation," I say, raising my voice. "We had too many toys and never learned to care for any of them, because everything can be replaced—replaced by another second-best something that leaves us forever unsatisfied."

Ophelia looks at me in horror, but I cannot stop.

"Who knows these days what he wants: this, this and this—maybe some of that. Doesn't matter because you'll be parting with it before long. It'll go into the charity bin in the parking lot, then on to some thrift shop where someone, with far fewer preferences to exercise, will pay for it with the last of his pennies."

Ophelia's expression changes to awe.

"A man of distinction is a hated animal today indeed, vain, elitist, snob. Better the morals of a man who takes what he is given again and again, but such a man is unhappy because he has put nothing of himself into the things he collects. His off-the-rack morals don't fit. Go to, never mind the whole damned thing. It has made me mad. Good-bye!"

"*Hamlet*? What's wrong with you? Are you nuts?"

I hear Ophelia's voice calling after me, like the little ewe's thin voice in the rain, and I run faster and faster until she is far behind me and heard no more.

September 24, 2009. For the past few days or so I have continued to amaze family and friends, who are now thoroughly certain I am mad. I am still in the tree house, although it's getting unseasonably cool. I switched the screen shutters for solid wooden ones, but it's been in the forties twice, so it was necessary to bring over three down comforters from the house. Often I make a fire in a pit that I dug a few yards off from the tree house. I get warmed up there before heading up the trunk to bed, taking two hot stones with me. So far so good, but it can't go on, and I may have to go, barbed tail between my legs, back to the attic.

A frost was coming, so earlier in the week I helped Gertrude pull up the vulnerable tomato vines that were growing in a low spot, which still had a lot of green fruit on them. We hung them by the roots in the green house. We dug out the beets too and laid them by in the root cellar in pots filled with sand. We stored some of the summer squash and bins of apples in the dugout shed. Claudius does not take part in these rituals. He is fine with grocery store stuff.

He complains to Gertrude that she spends too much time at menial tasks, when she could just pay some Guatemalan to do it.

I think she's starting to realize he's an idiot. But what can she do now?

I took the train to stay with Horatio in Brooklyn a couple of nights. I had imagined him living with an equally attractive partner in one of those comfortable old brownstones surrounded by an extensive art book collection. Sadly, I found he had a bachelor's apartment in a big brick high-rise with a forlorn lobby and a graffitied elevator. He says he doesn't mind that he was fired from teaching; it gave him the chance to go back to get his engineering degree, but now that that's done, he hasn't found a job that pays well enough to get out of debt. He suspects he may have been blacklisted. Not sure if I can believe that or not.

One night after dinner in Manhattan, we walked the Brooklyn Bridge home. We went at a fairly good clip because the wind was pretty terrific. There was no moon, but the sky was clear. The scene was so different from the last time that we crossed that bridge together that we hardly thought of it, and said nothing about it. I looked for stars, but found none, obscured by the glow of the city. Horatio was surprised that I had not talked to my mother yet. I just want to be rid of Claudius, not change the world. He doesn't understand. I couldn't imagine Claudius knowingly being any part of a conspiracy, not him or any of those soft-bellied engineers he brings round for wine and pasta. But Horatio thinks I should consider the possibility that they were forced to do the work and wrote a bad report on purpose. I don't think so.

But anyway, we made some plans.

Horatio is on his way up to Amenia again. I am picking him up at the Wassaic train station, a lonely and picturesque place, newly constructed and fairly well done, with a red umber metal roof over the platform, wrought iron lamp posts and a quite wonderful, if homey, bronze statue of a small herd of Borden cows, about six or seven, ruminating over the demise of their fortunes. The station is situated along Route 22 in the middle of an otherwise empty windswept valley bottom, with the steep Wassaic hills close on either side. "Wassaic," the name of a tiny old hamlet in the town of Amenia, means "difficult pass" in the native tongue. When Gertrude and I first drove by this place, back when we came up with Polonius to look at the farm, we both saw the station and said "how cute" together. It reminded us of a toy German train set, and there was something inexplicably romantic about its being the last stop. This breathtaking little valley was our destination, we felt.

I wait on the platform, and the train comes rolling swiftly in and stops, placing the door at which Horatio stands looking out the window right in front of me. We smile and wait for the doors to open. It is good to see him. I haven't had a good friend in a very long time. We are both wearing black hoodies. His is under a tweed jacket. He carries a backpack and his old leather satchel. Later I am to drive him up to Poland where he has friends to stay with. I offered him the spare hammock in my tree, but he declined and tried to talk me into coming with him.

First we go to the farm and wait in the tree house for Gertrude and Claudius to leave. At about nine, they are finishing dinner. We climb down the ladder and put our hoods up. From the parking area we can see the big dumb back of his head framed in the window—perfect shot for an assassination, even a drive-by. We creep toward the house, aiming for the back door. Suddenly a stroke of light falls across the side terrace as the kitchen door opens. Horatio and I freeze. Gertrude pitches out some dirty water from a flower vase then slams the door. We run across the lawn, full of mirth, my old school teacher and I, like mischievous boys in the night.

"Are you sure they're leaving?" asks Horatio.

"They go for a walk after dinner every night. Claudius has some sort of bowel problem."

After a beat or two the porch light flickers on, and Claudius and Gertrude emerge from the house, dressed for the chilly evening. Claudius leads Gertrude down the steps, and they go crunching over the pea gravel toward the road and the rail trail a little ways away. Horatio and I slip inside.

My old room is sad indeed. The freshly painted white walls already show signs of abuse from the back of Claudius's Staples catalog desk chair. Over the hardwood floor he has installed wall-to-wall petroleum byproduct, grey. He has a white board on the wall, on which he's made "to do" lists in red marker. "Write bibliography," "answer CFP," and "buy antifungal cream" are crossed off and "get physical" and "fix short in stereo" are still to be done. He has hung bracket shelves on the wall—terribly ugly utilitarian things—on which stand black plastic binders, categorized catalogs of personal events and repair manuals.

The room is utterly profaned, my spirit completely exorcised.

Horatio powers up Claudius's computer, and we wait impatiently (PCs!) while it noisily boots. Finally, I am able to try what I guess is the password. When "G, E, R, T, R, U, D, E" gets us right in, Horatio and I have a good chuckle.

Thanks to the encouraging gods of contrivance, we find that Claudius is still signed into his e-mail. Quickly scanning a few random ones, we are able to confirm that he is just as boring as we imagined him to be. His e-mails to colleagues and friends contain the exact sort of chatter and facts that he disperses everywhere on any occasion.

At first we are disappointed, then I get a wonderful idea, an unbidden gift from the muse of mischief. "You know what I'm thinking Horatio; we could pretend to be him. Send idiot e-mails to superiors. See what happens."

"What if I wrote a bogus article in his name, and submitted it to an engineering journal?" suggests Horatio.

"Something like the Sokal affair?"

"Exactly," he says. "You know what I was thinking about the other day? This would be perfect. You know how Southwest Airlines has those old planes that are falling out of the sky? They'll have to retire a huge part of their fleet if they can't fix them. We can have Claudius come up with a repurposing strategy for the planes, suggesting that Southwest sell them to the Department of Defense as remote-controlled weapons." Horatio can hardly speak for laughing. "Explaining, citing the NIST report of course, that planes are even more effective than state-of-the-art demolition techniques or bunker busters for taking down buildings. You can reduce 110 stories to ten, giving you an all-in-one method of demolition and debris removal."

"Oh, that's perfect," I say with tears starting to come as the beauty and hilarity of this spontaneous plan crystallizes.

"Ordinarily it would be too stupid to get past the peer review, but his credentials will probably open all the doors we need." Horatio's laughing slows down and he sighs. "I can use all the details describing the plane damage to the towers almost verbatim from the report. That's sure to put the editor to sleep and off guard."

"We have to think of a really good title," I say, and in a moment I've got it. "How about 'A Modest Proposal for Effective Use of Airline Surplus for Urban Deployment: preventing aging fleets from being a burden to the airlines and instead allowing them to be a benefit for the public' something like that."

We crumple over in fits of hysterics. Then Horatio thinks he hears something. "Sh," he says. "What's that?"

I listen. "Nothing. Just a mouse. The Swiftian reference won't give us away?" I ask.

"Doubtful. Most engineers skipped eighteenth century English literature."

"Then, assuming the article is accepted," I say, "we wait until it's been out a day or two, then we reveal it as a hoax."

"Oh, won't Claudius be pissed!"

"Claudius? It's Gertrude I worry about," I say.

"But he can't get into any trouble about it. The journal might. We can get into trouble, I suppose."

"Who knows, maybe those sociopaths admire gumption, if I have my Hollywood conventions right. When do you think you can have this done, Horatio?"

"Pretty quickly—maybe ten days, two weeks. A lot of it can be copied and pasted from the report. I can change it up slightly, but no one has read that report, except truthers maybe. This is going to be fun, a parody of NIST. It's almost already a parody of itself. I will hardly have to change a thing."

"We'll have to be very careful how we communicate with the journal. We can write to the editor from this computer, but we will need to keep an eye on his e-mail."

"Even if he sees it, he'll probably just erase it as spam or something. Check his spam folder."

We close the computer down, get out of the house, and are climbing our tree when Claudius and Gertrude walk past, Claudius getting out one last toot or two as he follows ten paces behind Gertrude.

October 24, 2009. I am in a great mood, manic. In a week Horatio finished the article. He got the puffed-up monotone style of the NIST report perfectly. He backed up the argument with vast appendices—that would be omitted from the print journal, available online—which merely reproduced the data from NIST.

Our fears about getting caught before publication were soon allayed as the editor of *Engineering Now* wrote back very encouragingly within ten days! As luck would have it, Claudius and Gertrude had gone out for a movie, and I was on his computer again when the e-mail reply came in. The deferential junior editor had already read the paper and was notifying Claudius that he was sending it on to three reviewers. He promised a definite reply within a week, but as far as he was concerned the reviewers might ask for an additional clarification or two, but he was convinced of the argument.

I decided to try to get copies of all his incoming mails forwarded to another e-mail address that I created. I got that done and was closing the computer down just as Gertrude and Claudius came in the door. I slipped out the back before they came into the hall.

The editor's reply came one week to the day. One of the three reviewers had apparently recognized Horatio's paper as crap and rejected it without showing any willingness to suggest corrections, but the editor, having already expressed his enthusiasm to the distinguished author, felt insulted by the reviewer's audacity to question his judgment and sent it to a fourth reviewer with a cautionary note that two reviewers *and he* had already accepted it, with minor revisions. A few days later, the fourth reviewer, accordingly, approved it for publication. The print version would be out in three months, and the online edition would be available almost immediately.

In a few days, Horatio will do a live interview on an alternative media show revealing the hoax. I am looking forward, giddy as can be.

Meanwhile, it has become far too cold for me to remain holed up in the tree house. We've had three inches of early snow, and even the sheep have moved to winter quarters, spending their time in the dry cozy barn, bleats muffled by bales of hay. I, too, have gone indoors. One night last week my cold feet kept me awake. The hot stones I was taking to bed with me were turning cold before I could fall asleep. So I bundled up my blankets and went down the ladder. It was sometime before two a.m. I opened the front door soundlessly and moved with my trailing comforter like a ghost up the stairs, past their bedroom, in which a cartoon carpenter was apparently sawing logs. *God how can she sleep?*

In my new room, Gertrude had my bed made for me, with crisp cool cotton sheets that made my stomach go up when I slid between them, like it does when you go over a big dip in the road. She had carefully reconstructed the scene of my old room, hung my pictures, stuck glow-in-the-dark stars on the ceiling, and placed my favorite photo of my dad and me on the bedstand.

In the morning, perhaps her intuition told her I was upstairs asleep. As she opened the door carefully to check, I peeked through slitted lids, saw her relieved smile, and pretended to be sleeping. How many mornings had she checked, I wondered, hoping I had come back in the night? I heard her go out with my wire basket to gather the eggs, and then I smelled hot butter on the skillet.

Claudius had gotten up early and gone into the city, so my mother and I were able to have breakfast in peace. I read at the table as I usually do, and we talked about all the apples that had to be canned this year. There were six or eight bushels, and they were small, so peeling them would be laborious. I promised to help as I always have.

Over the years Gertrude and I have spent many hours, adding up to weeks or months, probably, at this same big maple kitchen table, with our short knives and our peelers, preparing the harvest for winter storage and talking, just the two of us.

The table has many scars and pits, dark and worn down. It came with the house, along with three or four other pieces, like the Gothic sideboard and Gertrude's sleigh bed, which could not be gotten through the hall door and out of the house, which had apparently been renovated around them. The oval tabletop was made from one massive thick board. It has a sturdy center leg with crude, but beautiful, hand-carved feet shaped like human hands holding eggs. We wondered if the Quaker who had built the oldest parts of the house had made the table too. Perhaps not. Too decorative for one of the "friends."

After breakfast, Gertrude placed two knives and two peelers on the table, repeating probably what the Quaker's wife did this time of year centuries before.

His name was George Reynolds. He and his wife, Abigail, along with one of their children, a two-year-old girl, Caroline, lay in the old burying ground on Mygatt Road. I went to find them a couple of years ago, after researching the history of the house. The couple was side by side, under legible slate headstones, with the florid light-handed script of an eighteenth century quarto. Other, newer stones in the graveyard made of Connecticut granite had not endured the centuries of weather as well. Abigail's marker had fallen over and covered her plot. I found their small daughter lying ten paces northwest of her parents at an odd alignment. One would think they'd all be in a row. Stony ground perhaps. The child went in first, of course, while parents grieved in the midst of some epidemic that sent dozens of small children to their graves in the same year. The three Reynolds all would have died in our house. Their bodies were probably laid out in the "parlor," which is now our living room. George, who died in winter, was probably stowed in our root cellar a few feet under, with the bins of root vegetables sitting over him, until the ground thawed. Then Abigail was left alone and lived on after her husband's death another forty years.

The next owner was another young widow, a granddaughter. Left wealthy, she had Tudor-style extensions built, with stucco between the heavy timbers, doubling the size of the house. She was likewise long-lived. Gertrude, I always thought, would continue the tradition of these long-suffering widows, who died with that first and only ring on their fingers. They are rolling and moaning in the graves, probably, at the idea of a number two like Claudius living under the roof, lying supine, mouth agape, upon the handsomely made sleigh bed.

They were sensible people, the Reynolds and their descendants, they built their barns sturdy and laid out the house so the long roofline follows the track of the winter sun. They planted orchards and built stone walls. They dug the well deep.

"All that thoughtful effort is wasted on the likes of Claudius, who would be better off in a new condo served by a number of service contracts," I said to my mother while we peeled apples.

"Try to be nice," she reminded me.

For her sake, so long as we all are housemates (which shouldn't be too much longer if Horatio and I have done it right), I will do my utmost to steer clear of him, but I will not be nice. When he is home, I will stay in my room reading. If he is downstairs when I need to go out, I will climb out my window and hop down from the porch roof. The only time we will have to face each other will be at dinner.

October 31, 2009. Tonight, All Hallow's Eve, Polonius has joined us for dinner. Ophelia could not make it. I've been staring at my phone throughout the meal. Gertrude is not happy with me. Although reading a print book at breakfast is acceptable—and has even been encouraged throughout my life—she draws the line at electronic devices at dinner.

We have a bowl out for trick or treaters, but in all the years we've lived in Amenia, no children have come. They're all terrified that we will pass out healthy snacks. Indeed Gertrude has the bowl filled with little boxes of organic raisins.

"Don't forget to brush your teeth, Hamlet. Raisins really stick," says Gertrude after I eat a box.

"Yes, Mother. You've mentioned that before."

"Ophelia didn't go out with her friends?" Gertrude asks.

"Friends?" replies Polonius. "No."

Polonius has a terrible cold and he is misery itself, shivering, holding, with both hands, a steaming cup of special tea Gertrude has brewed up for him. "This helps Gertrude. I feel my sinuses drying up."

"Good" she says very enthusiastically. "In a few minutes you'll feel it on the back of your throat and then your ears will feel better," Gertrude mothers him. "I got it from the herb lady at the market. She says she's a witch!"

"Gertrude," says Claudius, annoyed.

"Witches are just women herbalists. You don't know your history," she says assertively. Good Gertrude.

She clears the dishes and sets out another apple pie she and I have made.

Feeling a sneeze coming on, Polonius hurriedly puts down the cup and blows snot into our good Estonian linen. "Sorry," he says sheepishly.

Gertrude smiles patiently and goes to get him some tissue.

"Well fancy that this subject has come up again," I say in her absence. "Here is a news item you might be interested in uncle." I tap on my phone screen until Horatio's image appears. "You remember I mentioned Horatio?" I hold the screen in front of his face. A title on the bottom of the screen reads, "Halloween Trick: NIST Scandal."

"Oh, don't look so sour my good uncle. It's a comedy, a prank, a bit of tomfoolery, all in good jest. Just remember we're laughing at you, not with you." Claudius reaches for my phone and I hold it behind my back.

Claudius's mouth makes a thin straight line. Polonius is still trying to warm himself by huddling around his tea.

"Well, shall we?" I press play.

Gertrude comes back with a box of tissue and sits down. "What's this?" she asks smiling.

"One of those alternative Internet shows," Claudius says.

I prop my phone up on a rolled napkin so that they can lean their three heads together to see the little screen. I watch their faces as they listen to Horatio explain that he managed to get a parody report published in a reputable engineering journal using fake calculations and bad data to support a fake argument. "It got past the editor and peer reviewers," Horatio explains. "No one has noticed, just as no one noticed how idiotic the NIST report is."

Claudius waxes purple.

"Now comes the good part," I say. Gertrude glances at me angrily. "Horatio interviews well. Don't you think?" I say cheerfully. "Handsome guy."

"I used the name of a NIST contributor," Horatio goes on. "It was his credentials that got the paper through. The problem today is that authority is convincing, even when the scientific method is completely disregarded."

"I wonder whose name it was he used. Claudius, can you guess?" I ask.

Claudius leaves the room in a huff, and we hear him fumbling for a light in his office, knocking over his "moderne" floor lamp. "Why doesn't the light in here work?" he screams.

I taunt Claudius, calling out to him, "How much mass fell over the side, Uncle? How much of the load was subtracted? Make any estimates? Gather any data on that? How much mass was left to fall on the cold part of the buildings? What was the amount of added kinetic energy? Got any numbers? I heard that scientists like to measure things and write out equations."

"Hamlet this isn't the way to—" Gertrude breaks off.

Polonius looks at the ceiling, as if trying to disappear, and slurps his tea.

"Wait, Mother, this is what Claudius and his friends say to explain the collapse." I grab my phone, locate the text and read, " 'The potential energy released by the downward movement of the large building mass far exceeded the capacity of the intact structure below to absorb that' (should be "it") 'through energy' (should be "the" energy) 'of deformation.' Didn't even check the grammar, much less the figures." Then I shout down the hall, "Ring a bell Claudius?" Turning back to my mother I say, "*That* is the $20 million answer. That's it, Mother. That's *all* they wrote about the collapse of the intact structure that killed your husband. They spent the entire report investigating questions no one needed answers to, like how Claudius's bolt does after forty days and forty nights of fire."

"Hamlet," pleads Gertrude.

"I'm serious, Mother. He's a fraud."

"I'm not going to put up with this," says Claudius, coming back into the room.

"How much potential energy? How much mass? What was the capacity of the intact structure? Numbers, Uncle. Give me numbers."

Turning to Gertrude, he complains, "He spends a couple of hours on the Internet and he's a physicist."

"Maybe you could just answer his questions, Dear, so that we can all move on?" Gertrude pleads.

Claudius sits back at the table and goes back to eating. Gertrude and Polonius look at him in wonder for a moment and then they, too, take up their dessert forks.

"I'm sorry Gertrude, this must be very difficult for you," says Polonius. "Has Hamlet ever been seen by a psychiatrist?"

"No, he hasn't," I answer.

"You don't have to be crazy, like locked up in a padded room crazy, to need help," Polonius goes on as if I'm not there. "Medication can smooth over the difficulties, put one on an even keel. Ophelia always was a morose child, ever since her mother died, you know, and the medication just takes care of that."

"Helloo-hoo Polonius. Over here. I'm right here. No need to pretend I'm not here."

He sighs heavily and wags his head side to side. "It would be irresponsible of me as a parent not to get the help for her. They really have come far. She's on Paxil," he goes on cheerily, "which takes the sadness out, you know. And quite understandably Laertes needs a little help readjusting from a very goal-directed life, with discipline day-to-day, to the chaos of civilian life. I'll give you our physician's number. Make an appointment for him, Gertrude, and get him to go."

"So you've medicated Ophelia, is that it?"

Red lights flash in the driveway.

"Ah, what's this? Claudius has gone and dialed 9-1-1, has he? Didn't think he had it in him."

"Claudius, will you help Gertrude get him to the doctor?" pleads Polonius.

Claudius grunts into his teacup.

Knock on the door.

"I'll get it Gertrude," I say. "Won't be long."

In the front hall, I turn and run quietly up the stairs to my attic room. I pack a bag, and while I'm slipping out of the window, the police knock once more. By now Claudius will be going for the door. I hop down onto a porch roof and then to the ground with a thud.

Claudius is letting the two police officers inside. Through the dining room window I see Polonius and Gertrude sitting as I left them, each holding a teacup.

Another set of flashing lights comes down the driveway. Two patrol cars for me! Well, I'm impressed. Whatever did Claudius tell them? I run around to the back of the house, down the hill and through the pasture to come up behind the second police car.

I walk over to the driver's side window and tap lightly on the glass. The officer, startled, opens the door and gets out of the car.

"What seems to be the trouble officer?" I say, remembering that that's what the beautiful people always say in movies when they meet the police.

The officer is stout and shorter than I am. The radio attached to his belt is crackling and beeping. "Domestic," he answers. "We've got it under control here. Go on back home," he says, assuming I'm a nosey neighbor.

"No need to be impolite," I say. "Just thought I might help."

"Sir," he says, trying to use the professional manner described in his training manual, recently memorized for the exam, "you need to go on back home." (A wiser cop would have said "buddy" or "friend.")

"Say, it's young Gates," I say reading his badge, pleasantly surprised. "I knew your dad."

He pretends I haven't said anything.

I go on, "He sends a lot of business your way I bet, huh?—if they don't go into the army, that is." Gates Junior isn't listening. "Well, tell him Hamlet says hello."

Relieved to learn that I'm leaving, Gates says, "Goodnight man," which makes him seem slightly less drone-like. There's hope yet. He and his partner, a small female, who has gotten out of the car while we were talking, turn and walk toward the house. All the equipment around her waist is too much for her small frame, and I am reminded, disconcertingly, of a belly dancer, hips layered with veils. They simultaneously put their cowboy hats on. Sheriff's department, I guess.

I wait until they are almost to the front door, then I run to my car.

I stand outside of Ophelia's lighted window, throwing handfuls of gravel at the diamond glass panes. Finally, I see a shadow and she opens out her window and leans upon the sill.

"Is that Hamlet?" she loud whispers.

I stand frozen looking up at her, no coat upon my back, head uncovered, and with a look so piteous, as if I had been loosed out of hell to speak of horrors.

"What are you doing here?"

"I can't go home," I say. "Let me in."

"Why? What's happened?"

"Let me in, and I'll tell you."

"Wasn't my dad just at your house? He'll be home in a minute, won't he? If he sees your car here—"

"Where's Laertes?"

"Out."

I hear Ophelia swearing as she closes the window. In a minute or two, the front door opens. I run up the steps swiftly, push her inside, and close the door behind me. I take her by the wrist and hold her hard. Then I push her from me, holding her at arm's length and study her face, committing every last detail to memory, thinking that I may never see her again. She is so much thinner, I wonder if she's been starving herself or perhaps she has been ill. Her face is not made up, and her features are paler and somewhat vague, as if touched with a light watercolor wash. Her hair is natural brown again and damp, as if she has just washed it. She looks at me like a terrified squirrel that wants to bolt.

The thought of losing her makes me shake and I raise a profound sigh. I back away without taking my eyes from her and go out the door.

Chapter Twelve
Behind the Arras

November 1, 2009. The next day I lie cocooned in my hammock, peeping at the ceiling through a thin slit in the canvas, which I've pulled tight around me, gently rocking with the tree and the wind. I got back late last night and everything was quiet. The porch light was off, a sign that Gertrude did not expect me home again. I spent the night freezing, wrapped only in the thin skin of my hammock, and today the wind, though warmer, is damp and chills me to my bones.

I jump as heavy footsteps climb the ladder. "Hey Hamlet, are you there?" call Rosencrantz and Guildenstern.

"Part of me," I croak, heart pounding.

I pull myself up and stick my head out of my cocoon. Even in the dim light, I can see that they are both much thinner. They come in wearing the uncertain smiles of dogcatchers, not sure I won't bite.

I have not seen them for weeks. Facial definition has emerged from years of chubby formlessness. They are even good-looking men, though wearier now, much older. Their weight loss has left them with deep creases in the folds from their nose wings to the corners of their mouths, so that their mouths are now snoutlike. Their ears protrude, and between their brows are deep angry quote marks.

"I thought you two had gone to hell already."

"We went for training. But we're shipping out tomorrow," says Rosencrantz. He holds up a six-pack for me to see.

"Gertrude called us and asked us to talk to you before we left," says Guildenstern taking one of the beers. "She is really upset and wants you to come back into the house. She says to tell you that Claudius has gone out."

"I saw him leave," I reply.

"Well, then go in and talk to your mother," says Guildenstern.

"Is this a trick?" I ask. "No, I don't want a Miller Lite."

"I hear you're the one playing tricks," says Guildenstern. "Why would you do that?"

"To embarrass Claudius, make him lose his job?" asks Rosencrantz.

"To avenge my father's murder."

"Claudius had nothing to do with your father's death. If you want to avenge his murder then you should sign up with us."

"Geez guys, no. I feel sorry for that idiot. I feel sorrier for my mum!"

They look at each other. "We don't understand," says Guildenstern.

"Hamlet, I'm just saying your mother wants to talk to you. She's pretty upset."

"Tell her I'm coming."

Gertrude sits at the kitchen table weeping. She has placed the wastepaper basket from the front hall powder room at her feet, and it is half filled with balls of tissue. The tissue box, the same one she had retrieved the evening before for Polonius, sits on the table next to Claudius's copy of the towers report.

"I don't understand," she says as soon as I walk in.

"That's not surprising. It's meaningless," I say, looking at the report.

"He's proud of that work," she says, sniffling.

"What makes you think he's proud? *You* were proud of him. The problem with you, Mother, is you don't understand mediocrity. He isn't interested in greatness or doing the right thing. He does what he's told. And he likes his benefits too much."

She looks at me like she doesn't know what I'm talking about.

"You, Mother, his promotion."

"No."

"They blew up, Mom. The buildings blew up. They knew the planes were coming. They let it happen, and they were ready with their pyrotechnics. Might as well take full advantage. They couldn't be satisfied with damaged buildings or hundreds dead; they wanted them to go, gloriously, down; they wanted something *big*." Changing to sarcasm, I add with a smile, "And might as well work in an urban renewal plan. Need to please all interested parties. Thrift is a virtue, after all!"

I bring out my bag of dust and hold it in front of her face. "This, Mother, this is the dust that I collected that day."

"What are you talking about?" she asks, her light Danish eyes wild and her hand smoothing her blonde hair that is all askew.

"Dust, the dust that was everywhere. They cleaned up and carted it off pretty fast. But I picked up a handful and kept it. Well I didn't keep it, but Horatio kept it for me. Do you know what is in this dust?"

Gertrude shakes her head, moaning, "no." Three or four giant tears roll down her cheeks unchecked and plop upon her shirt.

"Powdered concrete, lots of calcium, probably from the sheetrock, little tiny spheres of iron, and one-molecule-thin sandwiches of elemental aluminum and iron oxide, very reactive. Do you know what else is in here? A grain or two of some twenty-five hundred missing bodies. Maybe some of your husband is in this dust, Gertrude."

"Hamlet!" Gertrude cries and slides from her chair to the floor. "How can you talk of numbers like that?"

"Someone should. Didn't you ever wonder why there were no bodies, or hardly any, only splinters of bone, two inches at the very longest?" My voice is calm and mocking. "New York was peppered everywhere with bits of Dad. He blew away, Gertrude. He drifted with the pollution and fell upon the streets and the street cleaners came and swept him up."

"Stop it," she sobs.

"What were we thinking? Were we thinking? Why didn't we get mad? Ask questions?"

"I don't know. I was such a mess then, Hamlet. You know we both were. Don't ask me why I wasn't good enough at grieving. I did what I did. I don't want to go through it again."

"Did we ever really go through it or did we just postpone it? I feel like I'm finally feeling it. It feels good, Mother, to be in pain."

"What are you saying?" she asks, double lines between her brows.

"I don't know Gertrude." I sink to the floor next to her. Suddenly I am exhausted. Gertrude hangs her limp arms around my shoulders and puts her wet cheek on my neck. "I don't know what it means. Somebody did it," I say pathetically.

"What do you want me to do?" she asks, showing me the tenderness that I have been craving for months. Her running mascara has left two grey trails down the sides of her nose. Her lashes are all matted and she looks at me imploringly, childlike, with brows raised.

"It's happened. I have no idea what you should do. Get rid of *him*, of course. Beyond that, I don't know if you or I or anybody should do anything. People have to know. Actions may or not follow."

"But I thought Claudius —"

"I could have told you— Where is he, by the way?"

"He went to see the sheriff."

"He went to see the sheriff?"

"They called an emergency town meeting."

"An emergency town meeting? About me?"

Gertrude nods.

"Oh, for Christ's sake Gertrude. Why didn't you tell me?" I stand up and sigh. "I have to go."

"Where? Not back to the tree house? It's cold."

"Cold? To the meeting, Mother, to the meeting. Lend me that skirt."

I haven't grown much of a beard yet; I suppose that's lucky. With a little of Gertrude's makeup and a curling iron applied to my hair, I don't recognize myself. How the meaning of my features is altered with the change of context. I'm a little disturbed, in fact, that it takes so little to make me look more like a woman than a man. A little pink lip goo and longer lashes—and a dress—is all it takes. Although Gertrude's skirt didn't fit, a little tight, I found a stretch pink pullover sweater dress that works great with the leather pumps Horatio got me for my Cinderella costume. (Gertrude stood by wincing and whining while I tried things on, sometimes helping and sometimes telling me, "Stop this craziness.")

With a green silk scarf around my throat, I drive to the town hall, which is, sadly, situated in the back of the Volunteer Fire Department building in their rec room—a temporary arrangement that has gone on for as long as I remember. As I head across the parking lot, at first my shoes keep falling off, then I realize the trick is to walk on my toes with one foot in front of the other, as if on a balance beam, not off to the sides like a chimpanzee.

When I enter I can hear the meeting is just getting started. The long carpeted hall gives onto a large gymnasium where some court furniture has been set up: a judge's desk, which is empty for the moment, a place for a jury, which is serving as additional seating for the many townspeople in attendance. The jury seats are big, cushy, armless desk chairs on swivel centers. These seats are filled with people idly twisting to and fro like ADHD kids, leaving the rest of the crowd to make do with the usual banquet-style stacking chairs, the kind that lock together on the side, forming one long bench. (A maximum of two and a half seats per person please.) The room is filled. How did word get round so quickly? I wonder. Several Webutuck school board members, remembered from the good old days, stand behind fake-grain tables that, in times of trial, accommodate the witnesses, the court clerk, and stenographer. Two conference tables have been set up in front of the judicial furniture, at which the town board members sit with name plaques, replicating names on local business signs.

Everyone is standing with hands on hearts, passionately saying—practically singing—the pledge of allegiance. It just seems weird to me to see adults saying it. Although I don't see him yet, I distinctly hear Carlyle Hogg's voice lifted above the crowd's, emphasizing, "the United States of America" as if to bitterly dis every other country not his own. I slip into the back along the wall behind the crowd and join in, hand squeezing the foam boob of Gertrude's wonder bra, quietly saying "underdog" in place of that interloped phrase.

The town supervisor remains standing as everyone else lowers himself or herself cautiously. They either hang on to someone or place a forearm on the back of the seat to prevent all their weight from crashing down at once. There is no seat for me. Good old Booz, who is sitting nearby, jumps to his feet and offers me his seat. I smile flirtatiously and sit down. I hope he is not too interested: I did not shave my legs all that carefully. Keeping my head low behind the woman in front of me, I scan the room. I do not see Claudius anywhere.

The supervisor looks familiar. He pops open a Diet Coke and takes a quick sip before slamming the can down on the table and pushing up his glasses to read his notes. Ah yes, it's Ed from the Wellness Committee. He does not seem pleased about having to call a meeting on a Sunday.

I remember when Gertrude and I first moved to Amenia, we thought Ed's hardware store, always decorated with red, white, and blue banners, was probably owned by Arabs or else Vietnamese. But no, we eventually learned, it was a local boy, Ed Jefferson, who owned Jefferson's Hardware. He had three sons, one my age whom I befriended for a time, who worked in the store.

Every month, he and his sons lovingly constructed a new "Made in the USA" display pyramid in the center of the store with different sale items: tools, products, or building supplies. The precarious displays often represented feats of engineering, and people would go in to the store every week just to see the new work. I will never forget the hammer pyramid, which had to be cordoned off with yellow caution tape. People in town still talk about that one.

At the time, I think I dismissed him as a Republican and a xenophobe. I guess I had bought the "Kumbaya" rhetoric of the "one world" global marketplace without thinking about the Chinese workers who were being tempted from their family farms by the sirens of western entertainment technology. I had associated flag waving with bigotry.

What an arrogant kid I was. Ed is probably a decent enough guy, I realize now, who simply values a high-quality hammer, made out of strong wood and tough steel, backed by a lifetime guarantee, sold for a high-enough price for its maker to live decently. I think of my father's tools inherited from his uncle, which we still have in our shed. My mascara is running. Why am I so sensitive? Could it be the dress? No, I have been through a lot lately. That night, with Horatio at the barn party in Poland, something changed in me that cannot be put into words. The news of the explosives shattered everything, and then—with Easter in the rain—everything fell back together differently.

Out of respect for his office, Ed has added a tie to his plaid flannel shirt and blue jean outfit. He is consulting his notes and looking over his glasses at the crowd. The meeting is brought to order. He has studied *Robert's Rules of Order* and deals with preliminaries in the antiquated way of board meetings, yeas for yeses and nays for nos.

The first speaker will be Carlyle Hogg, longtime community leader who is now with the Department of Homeland Security. "Here to advise us," adds Ed almost sarcastically. Ed seems to have lost some of his admiration for Carlyle. I think I remember something about Ed having to fight against a group of locals a few years ago who wanted a Mega Mart to come to town. Hogg had been all in favor and criticized Ed for "price gouging" in the *Harlem Valley Weekly*.

Hogg stands. I see now that he has aged a lot since the Wellness Committee days. He stills wears the gold and emerald ring commemorating his performance on the Webutuck High School football team twenty or more years ago, back in the day. He has grown thug-like and unhappy: closely cropped head, dark green tattoo smear peeking out of his left cuff. His mouth is fixed in a scowl, and his smile is the expression of someone carrying heavy furniture. I think he has lost some weight. He wears a new single-breasted cheap suit over a white shirt that is too big for him, with a loosened red tie that looks to be thick stiff acrylic. I notice, when he adjusts his coat, that he is holstered under that jacket.

He clears his throat and speaks the voice of a longtime Pall Mall guy, "I think everybody here knows what's happened." He doesn't wait for a response. "The question is should we take steps?" He clears his throat again and clears it some more. He takes out a wad of tissue from his pocket, hacking up a hairball after three or four loud and desperate attempts. He repockets the wad, straightens his tie and goes on. "So far, it's true, the damage is limited. No one even knows it involves Amenia residents, and the reputable news outlets have seen fit not to mention the matter at all."

There is murmuring in the crowd. Ed lightly taps his gavel.

Hogg continues, "I've been investigating a possible domestic terrorist cell in Poland for the last several months. Hamlet is involved. That's all I can say."

More murmuring and several shout questions at Hogg, asking for details.

"Hold on. Hold on," he says putting out his hands as if to keep them back. "That's all I can say. You all know what goes on in Poland, most of you. There are a lot of people there, pretty well organized. As a precaution, I've been working with the sheriff on requisitioning an armored vehicle for peacekeeping. DHS is on top of it. That's all you need to know."

Mr. Gates has his hand raised, as do five or six others. I somehow find it weird to see adults raising their hands. Ed points to Gates, who jumps up like a jack-in-the-box and says, "I remember Hamlet when he was a boy, him and his mother. He was a student in the district in 2003. His mother is a know-it-all who cannot stand it when she doesn't get her way. It's no surprise her son has turned out this way." He sits down as abruptly as he had gotten up.

A dozen hands go up. Ed says, "You first Gazelle, then Holly and Hiram, and then Tom Statfor."

Gazelle asks, "Should I go now?" She wears a hoodie and plaid pajama pants tucked into faux-fleece boots. I recognize her from the scent of Tide detergent that hangs around her in a thick fog. Ever since Gazelle got back from Iraq, she attends most public functions. It's always the same dozen people you read about speaking up at the meetings. She uses a cane. I understand she injured her back in the war and is on disability now.

"Proceed Gazelle. You have the floor."

Somewhere to my right, a baby cries. I hear a woman's soft mellow voice say, "Sh, I'm here. I'm here." I lean forward to look. It is Kimmie Hogg with, probably, a grandson on her lap. (I remember that Kimmie's daughter is roughly my age.) She cradles the infant to her bosom and kisses his fuzzy head. She has a bottle for him, filled with chocolate milk. But he's had enough of that and is feeling quite buzzed. She offers him one shiny plastic thingy after another, constantly distracting his attention, trying to keep him busy and quiet. Finally, she takes out her phone and gets him to look at a video game. He'll be ADHD-ready in no time.

She was always such a meek woman, that Kimmie, and probably she doesn't mean to sabotage children's futures and metabolisms. Maybe I was too hard on her in my notes. I remember she could hardly get her voice up loud enough to be heard and was always so deferential to that monster husband of hers, wincing and flinching under his brutal hugs and other public displays of affection.

Carlyle Hogg has interrupted again and Ed has to remind him it's Gazelle's turn.

Gazelle, staying seated, straightens her back to get a little more height. "The other day I was at the four-way stop, and Gertrude comes along in that Prius of hers and just went on through out of turn. That says something about her and who she is as a person."

"Come on Gazelle," says Hiram. "That's not relevant." Hiram is a friend of my mother's. He's an enormous man on a motorized scooter, a worn, weathered mountain, with immovable legs like landslides propped out in front of him. I recognize his pleasantly smiling face, his asthmatic wheeze, and the same soiled shirt (from better days) whose buttons strive to keep things together.

Gazelle brusquely retorts, "I think it is. Those people moved in here like they own the town. From the very beginning that woman got in everyone's business. I'm not surprised her son has turned out so bad."

Holly Burton—I remember poor Ariel's mother—hoists herself up with the help of the man sitting next to her. She has another complaint about Gertrude. The meeting goes on like this for a while, with everybody reading off Gertrude's sins, large and small, from the great book of life.

Only Hiram comes to her defense. "I've known Gertrude for five years now. Me and my wife do wool processing for her at home. She pays cash."

"Sounds like she is taking advantage of your situation," says a crow-like voice in the back.

"She probably breaks even after feeding the sheep through winter," says a man sitting near me who looks like a farmer, with a brown, leathered face and shovel-sized hands. "No money in wool," he mumbles.

"Still she's taking advantage," says that voice again from the back.

"She isn't." Hiram insists. Then he says with a chuckle, "The worst thing she ever does is make me and Ida promise to watch PBS or listen to music when we pick the wool instead of watching regular TV."

"That PBS is nothing but propaganda," says Gazelle.

Hiram shrugs. "I don't know. We don't ever watch it."

The crowd laughs.

Tom takes the floor and begins by mentioning something about me (his stepdaughter, Belle, and I were on a soccer team together a few years ago) but then he digresses widely onto other topics, the coach, what color the uniforms were and why.

All the while, Ed is politely nodding. Some have taken out their phones and are making good use of their time. Tom rambles on. Out of nervousness he seems to have lost his way. He is still going on about the uniforms. Hogg is getting antsy. I can hear him twisting in his seat, sighing "uh," looking around him, rolling his eyes at anyone whose attention he can capture. Finally Hogg asks Ed to move on. Tom is embarrassed slightly and sits down. Glancing over his shoulder, Tom catches my eye and a quizzical expression comes over his face.

Hogg gets up again this time with a sheet of paper in his hand. "The Department of Homeland Security has done some studies on how to deal with situations like this. We know from research that," he begins reading, "anyone who has conspiracy theories or believes that the CIA is responsible for 9/11 might be potentially hostile to the federal government." He looks up from his paper momentarily, saying, "Obviously." Then he continues reading, "likewise for groups that show undue reverence for autonomy, disrespect authority, or have an unnatural interest in single causes, such as antinuclear energy or organic farming." Looking at the audience, he puts the paper back in his pocket. "Now we aren't saying he is guilty, *but* prevention is the key when it comes to terrorism. We can't have anything like that happen again, and it is sure not going to start in Amenia."

Booz raises his hand. Hogg calls on him. Poor Ed has lost control of the meeting. "What do we know about his father?" asks Booz. "He died on 9/11, right?"

"I heard that he didn't work in the towers," says Holly.

"What was he doing there?"

"I think he was a history professor," says Hiram.

"So what about this government guy from the city? Is he a weekender?" asks Booz.

"Her new husband?" asks Ed for clarification.

"Yeah, the guy that had his identity stolen by Hamlet."

"It wasn't her son, Hamlet, that wrote the paper. It was some queer fellow, his friend, that did it," says Hogg.

"That Hamlet was a troublemaker at eleven," says Gates.

Hiram asks, "How do we know the boy's wrong?"

"What are you talking about?" snaps Hogg. "Of course he's wrong. Did you see anything about this on the real news? Not a word! That's because he's some stupid punk. If there was any truth to it, it would have been all over the news."

"The only reason why we heard of this is because the sheriff was called out," explains Ed.

"That boy is obviously nuts," says Gazelle. "Some kind of delusionary thinking. Who's next? They always had it out for you, Carlyle. Insulted your wife and all."

Hogg starts to redden. You can tell he's already gone through this in his mind. Years of smoldering revenge are finally finding an outlet. "That Gertrude was obviously mentally unbalanced," he says. "Obviously it runs in the family."

Cut to a lynching scene, Cinderella shoes dangling from my toes at eye level with the crowd, Gazelle holding the torch.

No, actually I don't see that happening here in Amenia. They are all just bored, basically, not evil. Glad to have some excitement. This town meeting will give them plenty to talk about for months. No need to waste energy looking for a strong rope, finding a suitable tree, and figuring out how to tie a noose. So I'm a "conspiracy theorist"; no one cares but Hogg. They all just want to complain about what snobs Gertrude and I are. And Hogg really only cares for personal reasons unrelated to national security.

"I can tell you," Hogg goes on, "as an expert, that there is no way they could have wired up that whole building without anyone seeing something funny. Like someone's not going to notice explosives attached to every column." He laughs. "You know what a bomb looks like, even if you're not a specialist."

Unable to keep myself from speaking I raise my hand and interrupt. "What if they weren't conventional bombs like Wile E. Coyote might have used?" My female voice, for some reason, comes out in a Southern accent. Raising my hand has made my bra ride up. I try to pull it back down discreetly.

"Doesn't matter, Honey" says the Lord of Misrule. "I can have him arrested just for suspicion of terrorism under the AUMF."

If no one knows what that is, they're all impressed nevertheless.

Even though the meeting does not end there, and Hiram and Gazelle go on arguing about PBS, I decide to slip out after Carlyle Hogg's declaration. The others may be harmless, but Hogg is dumb, pissed off at my mother, and packing a gun. He was chosen for his various promotions, no doubt, for his short fuse and low IQ. They want a domestic army that's fueled by personal rage and feelings of inadequacy.

Ideologies and principles don't inspire the kind of violent hatred needed for foot soldiers of tyranny.

Outside the night has grown warm and damp, and a gentle wind is bringing more warm weather from the west. The warmth stirs my heart like a daffodil bulb, or perhaps it's an endorphin-induced euphoria from the stress. I wipe off the lip goo with the back of my hand. I decide to leave my car at the town hall, to confuse them maybe, I don't know, maybe I just need air. I go up Mechanic Street toward the rail trail. I walk past section-eight housing, an old[h] nineteenth century general store and warehouse that have been divided into too many apartments, judging from the number of meters dotting the side. A mentally disabled old man wearing a schoolmarm Christmas sweater, sits on the lighted stoop, as always, waves and says hello too loudly. I wave back like I always do when I see him, which is pretty much every day, and he, as always, seems shocked to be acknowledged. Behind me I hear voices in the parking lot, car doors slamming. The meeting is letting out. I slip off my women's shoes and walk a little faster. Now that they've had their chance to share the gossip, they'll go home, have a starchy snack before bed and dream happily of winning the lottery, or flying, or beating Gertrude at arm wrestling. I turn onto the rail trail toward home.

The overhanging trees here are thick, growing up steep slopes on either side so that the trail here runs through a fairly deep valley. There is no moon now, and I cannot see my hand in front of my face. I step on something nasty, probably fox scat, and rub my bare foot clean on the grass.

It's not too far to home, only a ten-minute walk or so, but the darkness is so oppressive I can almost feel its feathery weight on my face. I put my hands out in front of me as I go. I think I'm walking straight, but every once in a while I veer off the trail, stepping off the asphalt with a jolt that makes my heart jump. I consider calling Horatio and asking him if I should drive to Brooklyn, rather than risk going back to my house. But I need to get my clothes and my bag, and I don't really want to leave Amenia anyway. Not now. Not just yet. Finally, I see the sky at the end of the tree tunnel, only a little lighter shade of dark, and I quicken my pace.

Then I hear the noise of an ATV coming up fast from behind. A beam of light stretches out toward me, and I quickly run off into the woods. I scrambled out of sight just in time before the headlight reaches the point where I was. I watch, with the other critters, the foxes and the deer, all our hearts pounding, as the vehicle passes. Surely the sheriff doesn't really think he's going to catch burglars that way. I pry my sweater dress free from clinging brambles and walk quickly to the road and onto my driveway.

When I climb the ladder to the tree house, I find Gertrude has brought blankets over. They are freshly washed in her homemade lavender soap, folded and stacked on the shelf, with a milk chocolate on top, just like the Swiss hotels we used to visit. Gertrude and I have stayed in some very nice hotels. I would like to be in Lake Como again with her now, where we went to grieve, or in Bergen where we went after, where it rained all the time and we ate seal sushi in the local market.

I get into my hammock with the fresh-smelling blankets surrounding me and reminisce about comforts and beautiful views and walks in fine parks. The sound of the sheep wading through fallen leaves startles me at first, but then I recognize their gaits and remember their habits. They like browsing at night.

I remember that we have an old driveway alert monitor in the garage, so I leave my warm nest to look for it. After rummaging around in boxes and bins for some time with a flashlight, I find it and put new batteries in. We did not use it much. Stray cats and raccoons kept setting it off, waking us up with a frightening electronic version of "Für Elise." Tonight I would rather be bothered by the occasional skunk, than let Hogg take me by surprise. As long as I have enough warning, I can slip out through the window and up into the branches, if need be, and then run over to the swamp behind the rail trail, where I know the paths as well as any deer.

As soon as I set the alert up and get back to my hammock, a cat triggers it. At least I know it's working. I chase the cat long and hard, ensuring that he will not return. After that I am actually able to relax.

The cottage is quiet, Gertrude and Claudius inside, still up I think. One light burns in the kitchen. The calm before the storm, perhaps. I lie in my hammock listening to and jumping at many curious sounds outside: cars speeding past, even a distant crash, laughter, shouting. I start to doze.

I distinctly hear someone coming up the ladder, and I am instantly chilled with fear. I call out, "Rosencrantz, Guildenstern is that you?" Nothing. "If that's not you, you better tell me who you are," I say sternly.

A head appears at the bottom of the door screen. I kick the door open, and there is Polonius's face, wearing a look of embarrassed surprise, as he leans slowly backward, arms trying to flap his way back to balance. His expression says, "I've got this. Don't worry."

I put out my hand anyway to grab his collar, but his shirt slips out of my grasp. He falls, twelve feet to the ground emitting a faint "ooh!" as he goes, landing on his back with his arms spread wide.

"Polonius you meddling old fool!" I shout. "What are you doing climbing trees at night?" I slide down the side of the ladder and crouch by his head where my hand touches warm blood running down the stone on which he has hit his grey, fragile egg-like skull.

I try to dig out my phone. Crouching as I am, I cannot get the phone out of the tight pocket. It takes me so long to get the damn thing out that I have time to think, 'When am I going to get this damn phone out?' Time seems to stretch, and I am overly conscious of my actions. I even have time to think that I'm overly conscious of my actions. Finally, I stand up and open the phone for light.

Polonius's mouth is open and his eyes half closed. He already bears the face of death. A smoothness comes to his skin, as worries vanish, his mind goes silent and relaxes. I touch his cheek and feel his neck for a pulse. He smells slightly of wine and unwashed hair. I call his name quietly this time, more like one trying to wake a child than wake the dead. "Polonius, Sir. Are you okay?"

He is not.

At last I think of calling for help and dial 9-1-1.

Gertrude, who heard me yelling, has been calling my name. She is heading toward me now, breaking into a jog, trying to get her arms through the sleeves of her sweater.

The ambulance pulls away slowly. Gertrude stands with me, both of us wrapped in the blanket that we had covered Polonius with. It's not so cold, but we both shiver. A deputy, the same Gates who had come the night before, stands with a notepad out, writing a report.

Poor Ophelia, I am thinking. Poor mad Ophelia.

The deputy wants to notify next of kin.

"Do you want me to call her or should you?" asks Gertrude.

"I can't. I can't."

"You probably should," she says gently.

"I've killed her father. She'll never marry me now."

"Hamlet," she says, disappointed in me. "Maybe not, but—"

"It was an accident."

"Yes, it was an accident and no one is blaming you. It's terrible, but you're going to have to talk to her."

"How can I? She'll hate me. I don't even know if she loved me. She never answered my letter. And I've been a beast to her. I never said I was sorry."

"She may need to speak to you, even if it's painful. Try to think how she is going to feel. She's only fifteen."

"I will send flowers and a note."

Gertrude says to the deputy, "He has a daughter, Ophelia, and a son, Laertes. I'm calling them now." She takes her phone out of her pocket and steps to the side.

Dear Ophelia, by now you've heard the dreadful news that your father fell off a ladder and died. No, that's not right. I'm not to start by repackaging the news in a way that goes lighter on me.

Sorry for accidentally killing your father by knocking him off the ladder. Honestly, I was afraid he was some sinister person coming up to the tree house. I threw the door open. You remember it swings out. Oh, Ophelia, do remember the hours we spent here. (For I am here still.) And now you will never be able to think about this little bird's nest without remembering the dreadful way your father died here.

You're in your bed now, I bet, lying on your side hugging your knees. There is a phantom rising up in your mind, a soulless golem who now acts my part in your memories, a vacant body that you're not sure you ever loved.

Your silly old father, you yourself said it often enough, silly and well intended. Meddling to the end, trying to come up here to give me a good talk.

Who would have thought a sick, old man would be stealthily climbing ladders up trees in the dark. I called out to him, but he didn't answer, the poor deaf fool. At least it was quick, and he didn't suffer, and he lived a good long life, lucky man.

My mother is as much to blame for sending him.

How can I think such heartless things? Who could blame you for imagining me to be a crazed enemy of the people. As you lie there, all cried out, hating me for being what they say I am. You can hardly believe we used to be friends, and you don't know what went wrong with me or how I could have lost my way. But lost my way surely I have, you think, because everybody says so. And now that I've killed your father, that certainly cinches it for you.

Oh, vicious Hamlet, how you go on about your own sorrows. The girl's father is dead.

I've become unlucky, and tragedy will now shadow me because I don't have the comfort of friends anymore, my world is unstable, and more misfortunes will follow, heavy like hail in summer. I have become feared, so I am fearful, so I become jumpy. I am jumpy, so I act without thinking.

As you lie in your warm bed—the light outside has sputtered from deep black to grey—you are still in your coat and shoes because you threw yourself sobbing on the bed without bothering to take them off. As you lie there, please try to imagine that this tragedy is bigger than we even imagine and it goes on hurting people. I lost a father. Now I lost my future father-in-law. No that's not right. Cannot call attention to how I suffer by killing Claudius, I mean by accidentally killing Polonius. Beast down.

You and your father have fallen victim to the madness that's now in me. I was just its unwilling tool. Truth is a lie because the world is mad.

Oh, Ophelia I am so sorry. Maybe that is all I should say.

November 4, 2009. At the funeral home in Millbrook, Gertrude, Claudius and I wait in the front pew with the funeral director and his wife who are both excellent at grieving; they really show us how it gets done. The director is very tall and thin, with long cool thin hands. He holds his head up high and doesn't blubber or anything, but sometimes, when he greets another family member, he loses control momentarily and has to turn his head and bring his hand to his face. Then he pulls himself together and goes on with his duties.

He has silver grey hair and his first name is Mortimer. You can't make this up. His suit is beautiful, a very fine silk wool blend from the look of it, a very dark charcoal. His wife, Alma, has a pleasant round face, very plumb smooth skin, ageless, although her hair is likewise grey. *She* is weeping, full on, like a proper wailing woman. Tears roll from one eye, then the other while she mops them constantly with a pressed folded hanky. Every once in a while she breaks down with a good agonized sob.

Am I to imagine that, after all these years of funerals, they two still feel such sadness at ordinary loss? You'd think they'd be over it, inured, calloused. Instead they seem to have gotten better at being sad. I envy them their pain. I am jealous of the sheer size of Alma's teardrops. Oh, that she had been able to cry for *my* father.

I, in comparison, am feeling as dry as an old root. Ophelia does not answer my calls. She turned back my letter and my flowers. Neither she nor Laertes have arrived yet, and the two dozen or so friends are waiting patiently. It is ten thirty-five and the service was scheduled to begin at ten.

Enter Laertes, carrying Ophelia's corpse.

I hear gasps roll like a wave over the mourners, and I turn to see Laertes, disheveled like a tipsy groom, suit unbuttoned, missing tie, about to cross the threshold with his pale bride. Alma wails with a sound like pure despairing fear, so cold and so utterly bleak that I don't think I will ever unhear it. Laertes carries Ophelia to the front of the chapel and lays her down on the floor beneath her father's open casket amid a profusion of lilies, white roses and baby's breath. She is wearing the same white flannel robe she wore the night I went to her window. Ophelia's bleached white complexion compares tragically to Polonius's false blush. A crowd of women rushes around Ophelia and someone yells, "Call a doctor!" My heart bounds up from that despairing place that the wail had sent me, and for a moment I hope, against reason, that Ophelia yet lives.

Laertes stands with feet apart and hands spread, looking around. Then he sees me.

"Brother," I say holding open my arms. But there is wild rebellion in his look. What happens next is dreamlike. I am aware of his body some five feet away, and then I see a fist growing in size at great speed. Blackness comes as if a hood has been brought down over my head, and I feel hot blood on my lips, and I realize that I'm on my knees with my face and elbows on the carpeted aisle of the chapel.

Gertrude is saying something about it not being my fault.

I look up. "What a great *show* of grief!" I yell, though my voice is choked and my nose is filled with blood. I stand looking at Laertes through blood-soaked strands of hair. "You bring her poor body here so that you, the great lion Laertes, can demonstrate your pain. *I* loved her. I *loved* her."

"The devil take you to hell!" he yells. Throwing his body on me, he slams me to the floor.

"You don't know what you're asking for," I say struggling, feeling as if a great statue of Mars has fallen on me. "Please get your hands off me. I am not crazy shell-shocked like you, but I have something dangerous in me!"

Claudius yells "Pull them apart" at the funeral home traffic policemen, who have been summoned. It takes four of them to pull Laertes off.

I find I am lying on the floor not far from the body of my poor Ophelia. I roll longwise over to her, take her in my arms. She feels strangely light as if her bones were hollow like a bird's. She is beautiful still. Like the last time I saw her, in the darkened foyer of her father's home, she wears no makeup and her hair, her beautiful chestnut hair, lies in long loose waves around her face. "Why Ophelia?"

I hear a few voices around me wondering "how?" and "what happened?" but I know without asking.

"I loved Ophelia," I say to everyone. "Forty thousand brothers could not, with all their quantity of love, make up my sum."

"He's crazy," says Claudius to Laertes.

"He's not himself," says Gertrude.

I lay Ophelia gently down and stand staring at her for a while. Then addressing Laertes I ask, "Tell me what you will do to show your grief. Will you weep? Fight? Starve? Tear yourself apart? Eat a crocodile? I'll do it too!"

"He goes on like this for a while, then he calms down," says Gertrude. "He's just upset."

"Laertes, what reason do you have to treat me this way? I loved you too."

We did not put Polonius in the ground. His funeral service was postponed. He is still waiting, pink-faced in the freezer, for Ophelia to be processed like one of her pet birds, so that they can be laid together in the family vault. I took a few more blows from Laertes until his grief lost its anger and turned to confusion and then to pity and then to sympathy. Laertes himself took me to the emergency room where, after my nose was pulled and taped, I was interviewed by a psychiatrist.

I cannot breathe through my nose; my mouth is so dry; and no one has brought me water. Our pretty young Mexican nurse does not approve of "brawling," and she gives Laertes and me the cold shoulder as we wait together for paperwork to be done.

We've both lost Ophelia and our fathers. Collateral damage, not targeted in the initial blast, they were nevertheless slammed by percussive forces of power and greed that radiate out from the center and grow in ever widening concentric rings, never diminishing in energy, instead increasing by the free energy of the conformity of some and the induced madness of others. I still have my mother, but Laertes is all alone now with his war nightmares, and that's all. They have taken everything from him, one way or another. The fallout is more destructive than the bomb; it goes after the whole generation, the first responders, the families of the victims, and their bystanders.

Laertes and I sit together on a bench while waiting to be discharged. They think Laertes should have his hand X-rayed. He refuses to see the psychiatrist, and they probably will not let him leave until he does.

Laertes keeps shifting in and out of different delusions. "I still see the glitter from the IED blowing up," he says. "I still see the glitter in her hair when I carried her out of the car. I still see all that."

I think his medication is not right.

"Did she leave a note?" I ask as gently as I can.

"No!" he groans as if that makes it worse. "She kept saying she hears there are tricks in the world. She said she doubted everything and didn't give a straw about anything."

In OED micro font, on page seven of the ten-page folded legal disclaimer for Ophelia's prescription, I imagine there is a warning that possible side effects may include suicidal or homicidal ideation. Poor Ophelia's ordinary sorrow (boyfriend is a cad, old father dies) was amplified by greedy pharmaceutical conglomerates. She was not the Ophelia I remembered. I kept looking for her, and sometimes I saw traces of my Ophelia in the things she said or the way she smiled, but I had a feeling, the moment that she walked into the kitchen with that dyed red hair and ghoul makeup, that I was already talking to her ghost.

"My mother says lamb helps fight depression, better than chemicals. All grass-fed meat has lots of serotonin precursors."

Laertes laughs. "Thanks. You think it was the meds?"

"Don't you?"

"I do."

"Are you still on them?"

He nods slowly, staring ahead.

"You should wean," I suggest.

"It's painful," he says.

"We can have a good long cry together. I'd like that. I need that."

Chapter Thirteen
The Readiness is All

November 8, 2009. Claudius and Gertrude sit at one end of the dining room table. I pace back and forth in my Cinderella shoes.

I wore one of Gertrude's black dresses to the double funeral. This morning, when I greeted the mirror still wearing a bandit's mask of double black eyes, I decided to go with the raccoon eye-shadow look that is all the rage with teen girls, as it was with Ophelia.

Everyone left me alone at the service. That was the general idea. Laertes, Gertrude and Claudius sat with Mortimer and Alma in the front pew, and I lost myself among the rest of the mourners. Now, after dinner, Claudius is eager to tidy up a few details that have been left hanging by these unfortunate accidents.

"Claudius has a very generous offer," says Gertrude like a bad actor.

"Since you seem not to understand the relevance of the NIST report," says Claudius, "I have arranged for you and Horatio to go to Gaithersburg and meet with Dr. England who, as you know, is the lead investigator, my boss."

"Ah, Dr. England. Yes, he and Horatio might get on I think. He writes parody too."

"That's enough. Dr. England is being very gracious to agree to see you, as a favor to me. Now I hope you can have the decency and the discipline to be polite."

"When do I leave?"

"You fly out of White Plains tomorrow morning. Horatio is taking the train tonight."

"Hardly gives me time to get my nails done."

"I suppose you'll dress like that."

"No, I'll probably choose something more professional. Gertrude, could I borrow that houndstooth-checked jacket?"

"No Hamlet," she says tiredly.

"Never mind. I think I can find something."

November 9, 2009. White Plains airport security checkpoint.

I lower the celebrity sunglasses Gertrude loaned me, which partially cover the tape on my nose, and ask, "Is that one of those radiation scanners?"

"Radiowave, miss," says the blue-shirted TSA agent with matching latex gloves.

"Radio*wave*, ah. You do make it sound harmless. All the same, no thanks. My mother won't even eat irradiated strawberries. I think that's wise."

"Sorry, ma'am?"

"Ma'am now is it? Only a moment ago I was a miss. Then my being amiss changed your mind. But you're right. I *am* married, and my husband doesn't like strange men looking at me naked. I'll take a pat down."

"Could you step to the side, please?" he says irritably, then shouts to someone on the other side of the security checkpoint, "Roger. We have an opt-out."

Another scowling agent walks toward us.

"A what? Oh, hello Roger. I've got a plane to catch. Can we make this quick?"

"Have a seat ma'am." Roger looks uneasily at my hands. My knuckles give me away.

"Calling a female officer? I hope so. To me it doesn't matter, meaning it's just as bad either way, but, as I say, the Mr. has scruples. He might prefer a lady does the groping. Men are funny that way, aren't they?"

Silence.

I raise my right eyebrow at Roger. Another uncomfortable silent moment passes for him, while he blinks once slowly. After a while a stocky young agent with ginger hair comes along, checking her watch.

"O, here she is. Not really my type, but . . ."

"I'm Officer Downing, I'll explain the procedure to you first—"

"Officer *Downing*? Your first name wouldn't be 'Pat' would it? Oh, it *is*. I can tell by your smile. Oh, how funny. You know I keep a list of people whose names determine the sort of career they eventually take up. It's not a long list, but I will tell you my favorite so far, an earthquake scientist called 'Waverly Person.' I'm not kidding, though to be fair it's probably pronounced, 'pier son.' Still it's funny in print. In New York City, you know, there is a street called Waverly Place. Imagine that. What a funny addressed letter that would make."

"Ma'am."

"Oh, right. Officer Pat Downing. Let's do it."

"Ma'am, as I was saying, I'll explain the procedure to you first." She snaps on latex gloves. "Throughout the process, your safety is our priority. I will be using the palm of my hand to examine areas here and here. For the breast area, I'll be using the back of my hand like this. Your groin area will be examined like so."

"You switched to passive voice for that bit," I say.

"You may request a private area for your personal screening. Since you're wearing a skirt you may prefer it."

"You might have to lift it up, eh? Yeah, all right. I've already denied the boys there the chance to see my nudie pictures. Don't want to give them a girl-on-girl scene. Oh, who's this? Two of you now." Another female TSA agent has arrived.

"Please step inside here," says Pat mechanically.

I step inside the screened area where there is a table and a small machine of some kind, about the size of a toaster oven with the GE logo on. "Oh, this *is* nice. Just the three of us. She's a witness, I guess, in case I claim Pat does something untoward while she's 'just doing her job'."

"You can put a gown on if you feel more comfortable," the second, older officer suggests.

"A *gown*? Oh, you mean like a doctor's office gown?"

Pat shakes her head. "Step forward with your left foot. I'll examine your right groin area. Now return your left foot and step forward with your right."

"This is not protecting my freedoms, you know. This is a violation—oh, that was quick. All the trouble for *that*? If you're going to run your finger along my vulva you might as well really make sure I haven't got incendiaries sewn into my knickers. It doesn't take much of that military grade nano-thermite to do some damage. What can you tell by that light little thump?"

Pat takes a strip of white paper and rubs her gloved fingertips on it. Then she inserts the white strip into the machine.

"Look guys this is all too silly," I say switching to my normal voice. "No more jokes. I know *you* can't help be absurd in this situation—. What are you doing there, may I ask?"

"Testing for explosives residue."

"Oh, like if I got my bomb together in a rush this morning and didn't have time to change out of my explosives-residued sweater? How lucrative was GE's contract for those machines and the test strips, I wonder. Do you know the government didn't even test for explosives at the World Trade Center?"

"The procedure is complete. You can retrieve your belongings—"

"Other people did, you know. They found evidence. Look, Pat, you're not really looking for weapons. Your real job is just to scare me, so that I'll be happy to have you stick your glovèd hand up my skirt."

"I know," says Pat looking me in the eye. "We all know. But it's a job. You see?" Pat smiles, weakly, but genuinely.

The second officer is nodding too. "We know," she says.

"Okay I get it." I pat her on the back, Pat Downing, single mother of two or three. "Hey, take care."

"You too," she says warmly. "Have a safe trip."

At Dulles airport I slip into the ladies room, look after my bruises and change into my jeans and sneakers, come out a man, before heading to the baggage claim, where there is a silent chauffeur in a dark grey suit and sunglasses waiting with a sign, "Hamlet."

I hand him my bag. My black eyes and taped nose do not disturb him in the least. He's picked up stranger secret agents before. The dress would not have fazed him, probably.

I am driven to the NIST complex, all mirrored glass and chrome, and discharged at the entrance, where another nondescript speechless guide in a dark grey suit makes it clear I am to follow him by walking away with my bag. We ride the mirrored elevator to what floor I don't notice. Then I am shown into a large windowed conference room looking west at the setting sun. The room is dazzling bright and hot like a terrarium. Horatio is already waiting with a stack of folders in front of him.

I hardly have time to embrace him and explain my black eyes before Dr. England comes in carrying a folder. I quickly put my celebrity sunglasses on. England closes the door so quietly that it is almost sinister. He invites us to sit while he remains standing, leaning against a corner of a table. His wristwatch hangs a little loosely on his thin arm. He is Indian. There is a slight accent. He speaks directly to Horatio. I understand that I am just the (crazy) boy who collected the dust sample. The meeting moves swiftly, according to some tightly scripted plan. I feel like a carved figurine in a Black Forest cuckoo clock, playing my part, along with the chauffeur, the escort, Horatio, and the doctor.

He compliments Horatio for his "fine research" holding up the folder, in which, I imagine, is a copy of Horatio's dust sample analysis.

He wants to appear friendly. I get the feeling that he is interviewing Horatio for a job, and I'm not sure now why

Claudius had us come. To duke it out, I sort of thought, stupidly. No, that is not how it will go.

"Give this very serious consideration," Dr. England says. "This is an issue that is more important than any individual career, whether or not you believe you are correct. Your theory will be subjected to intense scrutiny and criticism."

"That would be nice," replies Horatio coolly.

"You would like to be noticed for your work. I understand that."

Horatio waves his hand by his ear as if he can't stand to listen to Dr. England, who goes on in the same calm tone.

"If you believe that nano-thermite is a successful way of attacking a building, we shouldn't be giving people ideas how to do that. In the nuclear weapon industry, my field, by law you can't talk about the details. So we just need to be very, very careful that we don't do something really dumb in the name of science—or any other name." He smiles paternally. "We need to think about how we serve society, and our service to society is more important than what kind of name we make for ourselves."

I feel like a third wheel. England hasn't even acknowledged me yet. The room is hot and stuffy. I gaze out the window, at an orderly parking lot, some low buildings in the distance. The sky is turning a beautiful blood orange. Horatio looks like he's whistling a fanciful tune in his head. I can tell he is not impressed with Dr. England. "Go on," he says.

Dr. England smiles. He has reason to think Horatio is pliable. We are here to meet with him after all. That is what people do when they go to meetings like this. They roll over. Claudius himself had such a meeting once, no doubt. "I have recently given some thought to how I can preserve your good name. You've got a promising career ahead of you. Getting a late start—"

Horatio gives him a fake smile.

"My intent is to show that I have as much concern for your well-being, Horatio—and you too Hamlet—" he adds condescendingly, suddenly acknowledging my existence, "as I do for our national security. I can almost promise you, Horatio, that my contact at Homeland Security will find funding for your research options. In fact, I can give you two ideas for grants."

Horatio raises his eyebrows.

Dr. England adds, as if an afterthought, "Both of them would have to do with fire being the causative agent for the collapse of the buildings, and you would change research direction—" He pauses and takes a deep breath. "I have learned to appreciate the value of silence, even if you have superior data and information."

"So you admit it?" I say to the doctor. "Horatio is right?"

Suddenly, his demeanor changes. He does not like me. "Did you ever consider what such a stunt might do? Hm?" He waits for me to respond.

I shrug.

He looks at Horatio who remains impassive.

England pushes his glasses up and glances at his watch. I notice that his fingernails are buffed to a sheen. His hair looks like it's been trimmed within the past hour, and he smells vaguely of rubbing alcohol. He looks down at me, my jeans and my sunglasses, and arches an eyebrow. "Even if it were true, it would be a handful of bad people who got out of control and left it to others to manage the mess. Do you want civil war? Do you want battles on American soil? Dead bodies in suburban backyards? Because that is what will happen if you, and people like you, manage to convince the general public that 9/11 was an 'inside job.' " He chuckles. "Trouble is you don't understand what it is the adults do in Washington. You can't possibly comprehend the subtleties of the relationships we have with the Saudis, the Afghanis, and yes, al-Qaeda.

"You folks have no idea, no idea," Dr. England goes on, quite out of temper now, "what it takes to keep this country the richest, most powerful, most feared and respected nation in the world. You folks have no idea how easy you have it. Do you think they have TV and computers in every home in China?"

Horatio is looking at me wearing his ironic smile. Poor move, he is thinking.

Dr. England supposes I'm just another Rosencrantz or Guildenstern, the product of the standard curriculum, mainstream media and reality TV.

"You think I'm one of your domestic animals," I say. "Well, you're wrong. I prefer the wild to your feces-filled barn."

Horatio says nothing, but he is suppressing a laugh, proud of his best student. We both get up to leave. England straightens up and stands between us and the door. For a moment I worry that we might not be able to leave. This may be a one-way trip to Gaithersburg. But no. Dr. England is suddenly polite again. He says he is sorry to hear that, and he steps aside to let us pass.

"We'll be in touch, Horatio," he says as we go out the door. "I'll send those grant proposals for you to look at. Just have a look, you know."

November 11, 2009. After Gaithersburg, I took the train back to New York with Horatio and spent the night in Brooklyn.

Claudius sent a nice e-mail saying how pleased he was that we went to see Dr. England as promised. He said all was forgiven, and that I'm to come back home for a makeup dinner and light entertainment to follow. I even get my old room back, and he will move his office to the attic. I suspect that Gertrude has shown signs of disapproval, and his ultimate departure is imminent.

The next day, as Horatio and I creep along in heavy traffic—it takes four hours to go eighty miles—a heavy drizzle turns to ice, and as we go farther north, we enter the Ice Queen's land, branches glittering in the sun, evergreens bending with the weight of the ice, birches leaning so far to the ground they look like catapults about to spring. When it all melts, I think, the trees will forever be bowed. In Patterson we are held up by a tree that has fallen in the road. Some men in plaid flannel coats clear it with chainsaws that they happened to have in their trucks.

When we finally arrive in Amenia, we see that the tree house is encapsulated in ice, like a crystal palace, the doors and windows frozen shut. As we drive past it, there is a powerful crack, as loud as a lightning strike, as a great limb breaks from the cottonwood and falls to the ground, scattering ice and branches.

Horatio pulls up to the house. "If your mind tells you something is wrong, obey it," he says. "I will make excuses for you, say you've decided to stay with me for a while."

"Why plan and scheme and make such an effort to roll the stone uphill? We know what will happen, not tonight, not here, but it will soon enough be over. We must wait for it. We don't know how to do it. The answers elude us. We strive. We live by basic, sound principles. We do our best and we're kind —well not me, not always—but we are *often* kind, and providence and karma take care of the rest. The great wheel of fortune is turning even now, and those who are up will come down."

"You're not giving up? That's what Dr. England expects," he says.

"Not at all. I'm just going to ad lib from now on. Let it come. The readiness is all."

We get to the bottom of the stone steps leading to the cottage door. A great cedar branch has fallen, blocking the way, but the sheep have discovered it and are hard at work clearing the area. They crowd around, munching on the fragrant green. Norway, the new lead ram, stands on the stone wall of the terrace, chewing thoughtfully. I notice he has lately grown a hairy fringe of a beard under his jaw, like a Quaker elder.

Horatio and I watch them for a while in silence.

"Horatio, remember one thing. I am not crazy. I know that this all got away from us a bit, and at times maybe it seemed like I really have gone mad, but I'm fine, as fine as a boy can be whose father's murder he must not revenge. The whole world would eventually be blind, said Gandhi, if we kept that up."

Horatio pats me on the back.

"I've written it all down, Horatio. Maybe some day I can tell the story."

"I'd like to help you do that." He embraces me firmly, then holds me at arm's length and smiles at me, just like my father used to do.

I watch as he returns to his car, starts his cranky engine and drives slowly down the icy road. I bend down among the ewes, letting them nuzzle my pockets in search of grain. "Your grass is all covered up, isn't it ladies." Their breath smells of sweet cedar as I scratch their woolly heads. "You poor things. In the spring, I promise, all this white stuff will be gone. C'mon. Let me get you some hay for now." As I lead them to the barn, the ewes crowd around me like happy children, and the gentle, noble Norway follows at a distance.

Coda

Harlem Valley Weekly

Since 1913

Friday, November 13, 2009

Rosencrantz and Guildenstern are dead

Wassaic, NY Two of Wassaic's sons were killed last week in Iraq as the transport unit that was carrying them to their base was attacked by insurgents. The boys, both 18 years old, were graduates of Webutuck High School and had departed for Iraq just last week after signing up for a two-year tour. Both boys' parents expressed profound grief at the news of their passing. Funeral arrangements will be announced next week when the boys' bodies return home.

DEATH IN ARCADIA

By R. E. Peters

Amenia, NY Four bodies were discovered in a farmhouse near Silo Ridge after an apparent murder-suicide yesterday, involving a husband and wife, her son, and a Millbrook resident, a friend of the family. According to the sheriff, the 18-year-old son shot his mother, stepfather and his friend in the backs of their heads, execution style, before turning the gun on himself. The gun recovered from the scene is a Sig Sauer P229, the same gun reportedly stolen during a recent town meeting. A number of neighbors claim that the son had been suffering from delusions and frequently spoke of 9/11 conspiracy theories. A Homeland Security agent, who happened to be driving by the farm on a routine call, heard the shots but arrived at the scene moments too late. Some neighbors report that an unmarked black van arrived shortly after the shots were heard, and a team of investigators sealed off access to the property until the

Death continued on page 5